Awakening:

The Foretold

Nikki Thornton

Cover design by Meraki Cover Design
Book design by Nikki Thornton

Printed in the United States of America

First Printing: October 2023

ISBN 979-8375831602

Awakening:

The Foretold

Chronicles of The Foretold
BOOK 1

CHAPTER 1

The very first words I ever heard spoken were, "Well, hello there, little one." It was just after my Mother Tree lowered me down to a pair of adults. The descent from her canopy was unsettling. I was nearly completely wrapped in her branches with just a small opening that I could see through as her limbs grew long enough to reach the ground.

I did not want to leave my Mother Tree. She was warm and kind, and I had been with her since my inception, five months before, but she withdrew her overgrown branches, returning them to their normal size, leaving me behind.

My guides told me that those first five months were a period of rapid growth for our kind. By the end of it, I was the size of a human five-year-old. Despite having just been born, I was able to respond when those two then strangers asked what my name was.

"I'm Ella. Who are you?" I had known my name since I first sprouted from my Mother Tree, as though Nature herself picked it out special for me. I knew it like I knew how to breathe. It was innate to my being.

I'd always thought it was odd how human babies weren't born with names and, instead, their parents picked one for them. I considered that perhaps they were born with names, but as they were unable to communicate it, they eventually forgot their birth name and conformed to the one that was chosen for them.

"We are your guides. Your Mother Tree called out to us so that we may care for you after she released you from her branches," the woman explained. She had wavy blonde hair and wide set green eyes.

I didn't like the way this sounded. I knew my Mother Tree. I could sense her moods and her aura. She never gave me any indication that I would have to leave her while I was a part of her. I was not sure I trusted these supposed guides.

"Why would Mother Tree want me to leave her? Why do I need to go with you?" I was perhaps the most bull-headed five-month-old in existence. Maybe not. Maybe I was just one of very few who could actually communicate.

This time, the man responded. He was slightly taller than the woman and had short black hair with hazel eyes. "Your Mother Tree can no longer nurture you. She cannot help you to become who you must be any more than she already has. She has called out to us to guide you. To show you the way of the Nymph."

I already knew I was a Nymph. I just didn't know how to articulate the word. I turned to my Mother Tree and stretched my arm out until my palm lay flat against her rough bark. I had an overwhelming sense of calm then. She assured me that these guides were telling the truth. She helped relax me and gave me the sense of calm that I needed in this sad time. I could feel that my Mother Tree considered it to be a joyous time, but no matter how much serenity she provided, I still felt sad about leaving her.

And so I willingly, yet reluctantly, went with my guides. As we journeyed out of the forest, I was in awe at the sheer vastness of it. There were so many trees of different types and sizes. I became sad at the thought of leaving this place behind. It was exceptionally beautiful.

The terrain was very hilly, and I found myself wondering if we were on a mountain. The sunlight filtered through the leaves above so that the ambient light had a green glow about it. Every so often, there would be a patch of brilliant yellow air that signified a gap in the canopy above. Despite the hundreds of birds chirping and dozens of small animals scurrying across the bed of dead leaves that blanketed the forest floor, I found this place to be peaceful.

We had been walking for over an hour when it started to rain. It was a heavy, warm rain. The kind that makes you want to stay out in it, even though you end up drenched. My guides decided it would be a good idea to stop and rest while the rain poured down.

They led me to the base of a great tree. I was surprised when I leaned up against it. While I could sense a presence to the tree, it was different than when I was with my Mother Tree. I wondered if this was because I was leaning on someone else's Mother Tree. They are very protective of their children, so perhaps they didn't take kindly to strangers standing on their roots.

I tried to convey our respect and love for this tree, but my message went unnoticed.

"Why won't she listen to my message?" I asked my guides.

"Well, Ella," the female guide started to say, "not every tree is a Mother Tree. Not every tree is capable of the level of interaction that you have become so accustomed to."

"But I feel a presence in her." I looked up at the tree and studied it. I identified it as a beech, though I wasn't exactly sure how I knew that word.

The male guide responded, "Every tree has an awareness, Ella. As Nymphs, we are able to sense that awareness, and after concentrated practice, we can understand that awareness and have limited communication back." He put his hand against the trunk above where my shoulder was leaning against the tree. "For example, she has sensed a curiosity in you, but it isn't about her. She can feel your desire to know our names."

That was when my 'mother' laughed for the first time in my presence. It was a whimsical laugh. Very light and airy. "I guess we were so excited to meet you and to be able to care for you, that it completely slipped our minds," she said.

Her husband proceeded to introduce them. "I am Aaron, and this is my partner, Armeta."

I was starting to notice that they seemed to finish each other's thoughts. I wondered if they were connected like I was connected to my Mother Tree. Even being miles away from her, I could still feel her encouragement.

As the rain let up, we continued on our way. Aaron informed me that our last name was Birch. The idea of a last name felt weird to me. Armeta assured me that it was odd for them at first too, but it was necessary that they pick one in order to fit into the human world. Since they were not sure how to go about picking a last name, they decided to use the name of the first tree they saw.

Hours piled onto hours and miles onto miles. We were so very deep into the forest that I was able to learn everything about my guides that a human child should know about a parent, and then some. It felt awkward to refer to them as my parents back then. Even though I knew it was necessary to protect our secret, it took a lot of getting used to.

After traveling for many days, we arrived at their home. I was surprised to find that it wasn't in the middle of a forest. That was also quite an adjustment.

Us Nymphs were most comfortable in the forest. Unfortunately, due to the changing times, it had become very difficult for my people to live in forests, and so we had to compromise by planting elaborate gardens and keeping as much greenery indoors as could be considered acceptable.

That first year was the hardest for me. My guides, I mean parents, enrolled me in kindergarten and almost as soon as I started school, winter came, and I went into hysterics.

My parents reassured me that the planet wasn't dying, and neither were the trees. In the back of my mind, I knew that the trees were just hibernating, but I was in such a panic, I didn't listen to my inner voice.

I became good friends with a human child that first winter. His name was Garrett. He helped me discover the wonders and the beauty of winter after he found me crying and keeping to myself at recess. He taught me how to make snow angels and throw snowballs and explained how his mom told him that every snowflake is unique, just like people. I learned about sledding and ice skating, and he promised that when we were older, we could go ice skating, just the two of us.

I would forever be grateful to him for helping me through that winter. Perhaps that was why I remained friends with him now, some fifteen years later, despite the fact that I was technically not supposed to.

And these last fifteen years had been somewhat of a double life. One half human, encompassing school and Garrett mostly, and the other half Nymph, comprised of lessons from my guides and Gatherings with others of our kind.

I once asked my guides if I could bring Garrett to a Gathering. I had yet to see them look as panicked as they did then. They thought I had told Garrett what I really was. It took a while to calm them down and convince them that I hadn't. I then had to swear up and down that I had no desire to clue him in.

That was the first time I ever lied to them. I thought it wouldn't hurt to just tell them what they wanted to hear. After all, no matter how badly I wanted to tell Garrett what I was, I knew I absolutely could not.

At my first Gathering, I met another newborn Nymph. Her name was Emma, and she had a dominant personality, even at that age. She and her guides lived just a few miles from me and mine, but she was in a different 'district.' I later found out that this was a fancy way to say that she couldn't go to the same school as me.

Emma came from a forest in Europe. Her Mother Tree was a great old oak. It made me feel better when she told me that she also missed her Mother Tree. She didn't ask where I came from, so I didn't tell her. Instead, I listened to her go on about caterpillars and how destructive they could be to a Mother Tree. I got the feeling that her Mother Tree had an infestation, but I never had the courage to ask.

When I first introduced Emma to Garrett, she behaved exceptionally snobbish toward him. I didn't understand why because I thought he was really cool and nice. When I asked her about it after Garrett went home, she told me that he was 'just a human.' To this day, she still doesn't understand my friendship with him.

"How can you be friends with someone you can't even be yourself around?" she would ask me.

"But I am myself around him," I would tell her.

She had this hysterical look of shock and awe spread across her face. "You mean you told him?"

I was appalled that she thought this. I wasn't sure if it was because she thought I was capable of sharing such a sacred secret or because of the tinge of pride that mingled with the shock that danced across her face.

This touchy subject comes up from time to time— ranging from a bored, "Have you told him yet?" to a jealous, "I still don't get how you can be such 'good' friends with someone that doesn't even know who you are!" complete with air quotes—whenever I turn her down due to plans with him.

We had this argument earlier this morning when she asked if I wanted to hang out with her. When I said I already had plans with Garrett, she got mad and added onto her normal argument with a snide remark regarding his intelligence. Normally, I take whatever she dishes out and just nod and placate her, but I didn't appreciate her attacking him this way.

"I'll have you know we talk about a lot of things, and the conversation is usually much more interesting with him than it is with you!"

I regretted it as soon as I said it, even if it was true. Most of our friendship was spent hearing her complain about everything from the rude barista at our favorite café to the latest drama in her relationship with Owen, most of which she brought on herself.

She and Owen had been on-again, off-again dating since middle school, and there was a period in high school where they were constantly fighting. Owen was a good looking guy with blond hair down to his chin, gray eyes, a chiseled jaw, and defined cheekbones. A lot of other girls in school made eyes at him, and Emma was constantly accusing him of cheating.

After my declaration, she recoiled as though I had slapped her across the face, which I'd guess in her opinion would have been less offensive. "Well, if you like him so much, why aren't you dating him?" She paused, and I braced for what I knew was coming. "Oh, wait, you *can't!*"

Her words stung more than I thought they would. I always told myself that Garrett was more like a brother to me, but I was only kidding myself. The tension between us was almost palpable.

"Wow," I said, as sarcastically as I could manage. "You know I don't want to date him."

"I'm gonna go," she told me, as she stood from the table we were sharing at the café. "You keep telling yourself that and see how it works out for you." She turned to leave, and her short blonde hair swung as though she had intentionally whipped it.

I didn't stay much longer after Emma left. I had a final exam to get to across town, and the bus service wasn't always reliable. It was my favorite class with my favorite teacher, and I was excited for the intermediate class I was taking next semester.

My guides found it humorous that I was taking a Mythology class, but I found it entertaining to compare the human interpretation of our histories with our realities. They got so much wrong that it was comical, and I found myself stifling a laugh more often than not.

I finished my herbal tea and deposited my cup in the recycle bin, smiling as I saw the symbol of the non-profit that I got off the ground.

There were so many companies in the area that didn't recycle, so while I was in high school, I started a company to bring recycling to the entire metro area. It was during our junior year. Garrett and I had a business class together, in which we were assigned to go through the motions of creating a business. He humored me and let me go with my non-profit recycling idea. I decided since we had to do almost everything for the class anyway, that I would actually start it up. Garrett stayed with the company ever since.

As I expected it would, the bus arrived fifteen minutes late. Times like this were when I wished I owned a car, but I couldn't imagine putting my own selfish desires above the health of Mother Earth. Very few Nymphs owned a car, and most of those that did lived in the country and had no access to public transportation.

I normally used the time on the bus to review my notes, but this was my only test today—and an easy one at that—so instead, I spent the ride thinking about my upcoming concert with Garrett. It wasn't one of my favorite bands, but I loved hanging out with him.

While taking the exam, I found myself having to think about a few of the questions so as to not answer with the actual history. At one point, I had started explaining about Aphrodite's true identity as a peddler of potions and spells that often had dire consequences, instead of writing about her Goddess of Love status and the role she played in the Trojan War. I quickly erased the paragraph I had written and replaced it with the human story.

After I finished, Mr. Robbins, who preferred to be called Brandon, spoke to me as I handed him the paper. "Will I see you next semester in the intermediate class?"

"I wouldn't miss it for the world," I replied.

He smiled at me as I left the classroom.

I wouldn't say I was a teacher's pet, but I thought he liked having me in the class because I so actively participated in discussions. Especially when I knew he was arguing something false. Of course, I couldn't tell him he was wrong, but I had fun playing Devil's advocate. It was especially entertaining when I would counter with the actual truth and he wrote it off as ridiculous and impossible.

CHAPTER 2

I was glad that I had found an apartment adjacent to campus because I could walk to all of my classes and to work. When I got into the building, I opted to climb the three stories to my unit instead of taking the dilapidated elevator. As this was a grungy rock band we were going to see tonight, I opted for a pair of torn up jeans and a slightly form fitting, dark red 'off-the-shoulder' t-shirt. The shirt was purposefully made to look old and worn with slashes cutting across it in a few places that revealed the skin-tight black tank top I wore underneath.

I dug out my studded belt that was considered fashionable back when I was in high school and pulled on a pair of black and white Converse. I was just finishing tying my skull patterned laces when I heard Garrett knock on the door.

When I opened it, he smiled and wrapped me in a hug. I ignored the fact that it was a little too long and a little too tight, like I always did. I also had to make a conscious effort to ignore how good it felt to be held by his strong arms.

Over the years, Garrett had fallen into the role of a good guy with a bad boy façade. He was ruggedly handsome with the most captivating crystal-clear blue eyes. He started wearing his light brown hair unkempt during our first year of college and never looked back.

When he released me from his embrace, he noticed my outfit. "Very rock and roll, Ella," he teased.

I rolled my eyes and pretended to flip my auburn hair off my shoulder. I normally left it in its naturally wavy state, but for the concert, I took the time to straighten it. I even spent time applying dramatic makeup, complete with smoky eye shadow to highlight my hazel-green eyes and deep red lipstick, made to look glossy thanks to my favorite cherry flavored lip gloss.

"Did you forget to shave?" I teased back, stroking the beginnings of a beard on his strong jawline.

"Nah, I've decided to start sporting some fuzz. Do you like it?" he asked, looking hopeful.

I studied his new look while I considered. It wasn't what I would call a full beard, but it was too long to be considered stubble or a five o'clock shadow.

He seemed uncomfortable with my focused attention. When he couldn't take it anymore, he finally asked, "Well?"

"It's..." I inhaled deeply and audibly, "good," I finished.

He looked pleased, and I had to look away before my cheeks started burning red.

As we walked across campus we talked about our days. I made sure to leave out the part about Emma flipping out. Just as Emma didn't like Garrett, Garrett wasn't too fond of Emma. He wasn't one to voice it, but his tone usually gave him away. His hand brushed against mine a few times along the way, making my breath catch slightly, which I internally attributed to our quick pace. After I was done rambling about my day, I finally asked about his.

"Well, since you're the only person I know insane enough to take a Friday class, I went for a morning run, then met up with Tracy and Felicia for lunch."

No sooner than he was done speaking, he lit a cigarette and took a long drag.

"Maybe if you quit smoking, you'd actually beat all of the fifty-year-olds running your 10Ks."

Garrett started running on the high school track team during our freshman year. That was the year we were sort of distant.

The middle schools consolidated into one high school, and that meant Emma and I were finally in the same building. She quickly seized up most of my time between classes and insisted on sitting next to me at lunch every day.

Garrett joined us at first, but every time he tried to speak, Emma would suddenly remember some 'super important' thing she had to tell me. Usually, they were just trivial topics, and sometimes, she would mention something that happened at the last Gathering with our Nymph friends to further exclude Garrett.

One day, he just didn't come into the lunchroom.

I looked around for him before Emma distracted me with her drama. I always assumed that school year was the reason Garrett disliked Emma but never actually confirmed it.

I still made time for him outside of school, but even that was limited due to my busy schedule. Between my Nymph studies, community garden volunteering, and reforestation project at the nearby state park, I didn't get to see him often, which was why I was shocked to see him smoking before school at the start of our sophomore year.

"Did you ever think maybe I want the fifty-year-olds to beat me?" he retorted. "Anyway, Tracy asked about you at lunch."

"Did she now?" I asked with a raised eyebrow. I really wasn't surprised. Tracy had a huge thing for Garrett and always thought I was the reason he wouldn't ask her out. Adorable but oblivious, Garrett had no idea.

"Yeah, she wanted to know why you didn't join us. I think she's starting to get a complex that you don't like her."

"I like her just fine." And really, I did. I just didn't need other humans as friends. Emma did have a point, however small I pretended it was, about it being difficult to be friends with a human. It became especially tricky when I saw a poor tree that needed a little healing. I'd had to make up some pretty wild excuses to get in close enough proximity to touch the tree so that I could diagnose the problem and offer a small amount of my energy to help it heal.

"You say that, but whenever I have plans with her, you always bail."

"I think she prefers it that way, honestly. Besides, I bail regardless of who you have plans with."

He considered this for a moment. "You're right. Aren't my friends good enough for you?"

"I'm sure they are. I just don't have time for more friends. You know how packed my schedule is." It was even more packed than he thought since he wasn't aware of my Nymph responsibilities. "So, how'd you handle Tracy?"

"I told her the truth. That you had a class." His lips slowly curled into one of his sly smiles.

"Oh God, what now?"

"When I told her what the class was, she asked me if you were into Voodoo." His eyes twinkled with his smile, which only happened when he was incredibly amused or happy.

"What in the hell does mythology have to do with Voodoo?"

"No idea," he said with a laugh.

The rest of our walk to the concert venue was in silence. Our hands brushed together a few more times along the way, and the crowd was so dense once we got there, that he seized the opportunity to grab my hand and led me to our seats.

The band was just a local one, but they had a large following. We were packed into a tiny venue on the other side of campus that was usually reserved for theater productions. I was pretty sure its ventilation system wasn't meant to accommodate such large crowds, and it got hot and sweaty fast.

After three hours of loud music, sweaty bodies, and a smoky atmosphere, we were finally headed home. Garrett held my hand most of the way so that we wouldn't get separated in the flood of people heading to the various dorms and apartment complexes across campus. I imagined he would have walked me home, even if we didn't live in the same building.

My ears were still ringing when we finally made it to our building.

As he was saying good night when I made to exit the stairway at my floor, he brought up an old, albeit reoccurring, conversation.

"Tell me again why we don't save our money and just live together?"

I sighed, "It would get awkward."

"I don't think so."

"It would," I insisted.

"How?"

"Picture this for a moment. You come home with some hot girl—"

"Just how hot are we talking?"

"It doesn't matter. She's hot."

"Of course it matters! Are we talking model-hot or you-hot?"

I rolled my eyes. "Model-hot." I paused to make sure he wasn't going to interject with any questions about just how hot model-hot was. "So, you and your model come in, just as I'm exiting the bathroom after a steamy hot shower in nothing but a towel..."

"Oh. You're right. That would get awkward," he conceded.

"Exactly."

"Yeah, she'd probably end up leaving because she'd realize she couldn't hold a candle to your beauty."

Before I could fully register what he said, he kissed me on the cheek, bid me a good night, and escaped up the stairs. That was just like him. It seemed like every time he made such a boldly flirtatious move, he made sure to have a quick exit available and always used it.

And he didn't think living together would be awkward.

Finally in my apartment, I dropped my keys on the counter and raided the fridge, grabbing the first thing I saw. I scarfed down my salad as though I hadn't eaten in three days before collapsing into my bed and passing out.

When I woke the next morning, it was to pounding on my door that could rival the sound of thunder in the middle of a wicked storm. I glanced at my clock and was instantly grateful that my complex housed only college students whose late-night partying would mean they were much too passed out to be awoken by my rude visitor.

Bleary eyed, I pulled on my emerald green robe and stumbled to the door. To my slight astonishment, Emma greeted me with a smile and a cup of herbal tea.

"I thought you were mad at me," I said, blocking her from entering my tiny studio apartment.

"What?" she asked, as though she had forgotten.

One thing I'd learned about Emma over the years was that she rarely forgot things like what passed between us yesterday morning.

"Oh," she continued, feigning a flicker of remembrance, "that. You need to relax. That was nothing. Completely forgotten. Water under the bridge. Leaves fallen in the autumn."

I let my guard down, and she eased her way past me and toward my kitchen. "Please, come in," I said to the hallway, as I closed the door.

My tiny little apartment was barely big enough for the both of us to maneuver. She plopped herself at the small counter that jutted out ever so slightly from the kitchen, providing the only place appropriate to have a sit-down meal.

Two people squeezing into that counter area proved mighty awkward unless you didn't mind literally rubbing elbows with the other person. It also made conversing difficult. It was this last reason that caused me to sit on the edge of my unmade bed instead of next to her.

I supposed the main reason my apartment was so crammed, though I preferred to call it cozy, was because I chose to sleep in a full-sized bed instead of a twin. Despite my small stature, I found that I always woke up hanging off the bed when I slept in a twin. It took some persuading when I was younger to get my parents to allow me to jam a full-sized bed into my small room at home. After that, there was no turning back.

"To what do I owe this wonderfully early pleasure?" I asked. It wasn't like Emma not to speak whatever was on her mind. She usually initiated our conversations. I always assumed it was so she could control what we talked about, which was usually her life.

"Did you have fun last night?"

I smiled, remembering the energy of the crowd, the smell of sweat and alcohol mixed with the smoke of cigarettes and pot. I remembered not caring that a bazillion people bumped into me and watching Garrett's face as he shouted lyrics back at the stage throughout the show.

Then, I remembered our walk there and our hands brushing against each other. I thought about our conversation when we got back home and how he held my hand the whole way. When I remembered the feel of his lips on my cheek as he said goodnight, I decided I should stop reminiscing.

"Yeah, it was a blast. The band was really good, and everyone was going crazy for them."

"Did you hook up with anyone?"

A typical Emma question. She seemed to be perpetually concerned with getting me laid. I wasn't sure why she thought I needed her help, but whenever we were out, it seemed she always tried.

While relationships with humans were highly frowned upon, it was much less taboo to have casual sex with them. The main concern for the relationship wasn't because they were a different species, so to speak, but because when you developed a deep connection with someone, it was easy to slip up about something that would lead them to discover your true identity. And boy, did I know how hard it was to hide.

That was why I did my best to avoid meaningful relationships with humans. Garrett was my only exception, and I couldn't bring myself to break things off with him. What I didn't tell Emma was that I was also careful not to have casual sex with humans because that was really just one step away from not-so-casual sex with a certain human, who I wouldn't admit having feelings for to myself, let alone to her. She would have a field day with that nugget of information.

"No, I didn't hook up with anyone. It's horny Nymphs like you who have given us our mythological reputation."

Her face distorted with an emotion I couldn't quite identify. Anguish? Panic? Anger? It was hard to tell.

"Okay, seriously. What's going on? I know you didn't come over this early to discuss my sex life," I pressed.

"You have to be having sex to have a sex life to discuss," she pointed out. When I opened my mouth to respond, she quickly added, "And Edgar doesn't count."

I sighed. Edgar was my last boyfriend and my first to be intimate with. He was a Nymph from a neighboring city that would sometimes come to our Gatherings. I caught his eye the summer after I hit puberty. I was so amazed to be receiving that kind of attention that I became caught up in the whirlwind of what I thought was romance.

Normally, it was Emma who received the attention from boys. She would tell me all about her encounters with this boy or that boy. They ranged from Nymph to human to even a few Fairies. She spoke of sex like it was this great rite of passage that felt better than anything one would ever experience in their lifetime. When Edgar initiated it, I decided to give it a try.

The day after, I sought Emma out to yell at her for lying. It wasn't the most wonderful thing in the world! It hurt like hell! She promised me it only hurt the first time. I pushed and pushed until she finally admitted that it may hurt the first *few* times. She told me how proud she was of me and how I should keep doing it until it felt good, then I'd know what she was talking about.

The naïve freshman that I was, I took her advice. Edgar and I continued to see each other. Even when our plans were just to go see a movie, it seemed like we always ended up having sex at the end of the night. He was also one of the horny Nymphs that gave us a bad reputation.

To my delight, Emma was right. The more we had sex, the less it hurt.

One night, after being together, I murmured that I loved him as we laid together in the afterglow. The next day, he broke up with me. Turns out, it wasn't romance or love for him. It was just lust.

I hadn't had sex since then, despite Emma constantly throwing horny men at me over the years. Truth was, after Edgar broke up with me, I promised myself I wouldn't have sex again unless I knew he really loved me.

Emma's hand was in my face, snapping for my attention.

"What?" I demanded.

"You completely spaced out," she informed me.

"Oh. Sorry."

There was a short pause between us that almost allowed me to space out again before she finally got to what was bothering her.

"Ella, I don't know what I'm going to do." She sounded panicked.

"Calm down. What happened? We'll figure it out," I said, starting to get worried that she was in serious trouble.

"It's Owen. Or rather, it's not Owen. I went out last night and bumped into Arthur, and... I don't know."

I fought the sigh that was desperately trying to escape my body while also making a concentrated effort to not roll my eyes. Of course this was her big emergency. "What happened with Arthur?" I hoped I sounded as interested and concerned as before.

"Nothing happened!"

I stared her down.

"I swear. Nothing. Well, except... I mean, we did flirt. Quite a bit. But I could tell he wanted something to happen. He kept leaning in more than he had to. Finding reasons to touch my arm or my back or my hair. He wanted me. And well, I wanted him too. It was like I forgot about Owen and all I wanted was Arthur. I barely made it out of there." She sounded exasperated by the end of her monologue.

"Owen is a really nice guy. He really doesn't deserve to be cheated on. If you really want to be with Arthur, you have to break up with Owen first. He deserves that much. You should probably even wait a week or two until you start up with Arthur, otherwise Owen will probably think you were already involved with him before you two broke up."

I felt so bad for Owen. He was the perpetual nice guy. I couldn't imagine why they were together, given her history and flair for drama, but somehow, they were— and somehow, he truly, deeply cared for her.

"Why do you care so much about how this affects Owen? You guys aren't even really friends. Have you been seeing each other when I'm not around?"

She tried to ask her questions innocently, but I knew her too well. She was jealous. She thought I liked Owen and that I wanted them to break up so that I could have him to myself. It was all in her accusatory glare.

This was why Owen and I decided a long time ago that it was best not to let Emma know how close we were. She wasn't exactly the most understanding, and she did tend to have a problem with jealousy.

It was funny, really, when you considered that Owen and I only became friends because they started dating. And our closeness was a direct result of her tendency to ignore him at parties so she could be the social butterfly that she was.

"Of course we haven't, Emma. Like you said, we aren't friends. I just know how good he is to you, and I'd hate to see someone you care about have their heart broken. I know what it would do to you." Sometimes I thought I should have pursued a career in PR. I really knew how to spin it, at least when it came to Emma.

"You're right. I'll call him tonight."

I glared at her with a raised eyebrow, silently encouraging her to do better.

"Okay, okay. I'll go see him today."

We had another slightly awkward pause until I broke it. "Well, thanks for the tea and the wakeup call. I have to get ready for the Gathering tonight and then go set everything up for it."

"No problem. Do you need any help?"

I wished her offer were genuine. "No thanks. Aaron and Armeta are going to be helping me."

"Okay, cool. I'll see you tonight then."

"You sure will." I smiled and followed her to the door.

Once she left, I took a long hot shower. I tried not to think about those nights with Edgar, but it proved difficult. When I was finally able to push him out of my head, Garrett annoyingly filled the open space. I wondered what he would think if he knew I thought about him in the shower.

CHAPTER 3

As I was heading toward the stairwell, carrying bags loaded with various items for the Gathering, Garrett suddenly opened the door and upon seeing me loaded down with so many bags, he came rushing toward me.

"Thanks," I said, as he grabbed everything except my backpack.

"Man, these are heavy! Where are you going with all this... whatever it is?" He started to peer into the bags.

I grabbed his scruffy chin and lifted his head so he wouldn't look inside them. It wasn't anything I couldn't explain away, but I'd rather not have to. "You, kind sir, are too nosy. I'm headed out to volunteer." I finally released his chin, though he seemed pleased with how long I held it.

"Volunteer for what? To be a pack mule?" He smiled his genuine, eye twinkling smile at me. After a moment that seemed like ages passed, he finally said, "I was just on my way to see you."

My mind finally stopped getting lost in his eyes, and I was able to continue down the hall. "Well, I'm just on my way out, as you can see. I'll stop by later."

"Whoa. You're not going to invite me to join you? You always try to get people to volunteer. What on Earth are you doing?" He tried to peer into the bags again.

"You can't come." My head was racing trying to figure out a good reason to use.

"And why not? Aren't you always preaching that not enough people volunteer and that organizations can always use more bodies?"

Sometimes, Garrett had too good of a memory.

"Yes, well... This is a, uh... I'm volunteering at a... a women's shelter. So, uh, no men allowed," I stuttered. I avoided eye contact while I stepped down the last few stairs. When I glanced sideways at him, I saw the muscles in his forearm protruding from the weight of the bags. "That's why those bags are so heavy. Canned goods," I explained.

He eyed me suspiciously, and I prayed that I hadn't over done it with the canned goods. "All right. Have fun. But definitely come by tonight. I feel like doing something fun."

We arrived at the bus stop. "We just did something fun last night." I looked past his shoulder and saw the bus at the red light a few blocks down.

"Fine. I feel like drinking tonight."

I frowned slightly. Garrett and I hadn't been able to go out drinking in quite some time, but if he wanted to do that tonight, then I'd have to get out of the Gathering early. Normally, I hung around with my Nymph friends afterward.

"Okay. But would you mind if Emma came?" When he didn't respond immediately, I stuck my bottom lip out in a pout. The bus was rapidly approaching.

"Would you come if she wasn't invited?"

"Probably not. I already blew her off yesterday."

"Fine, then she can come. I'll ask Tracy and Felicia too."

The bus opened its doors for me to get on. "You may want to invite some guys too so that Emma doesn't get bored," I teased.

"Maybe I'm counting on her getting bored and going home early," he said with a wink.

I grabbed the bags back from him and started up the steps. As the bus driver began closing the doors, Garrett stuck his arm in the way, much to the driver's annoyance.

"Hey, Ella," he began.

I turned toward him. "I swear to God, Garrett, if you flirt with me right now, I'm going to kill you." It was a typical moment for his bravery, and I didn't want to let him have it.

A crooked smile spread across his face. "That's quite a big ego you got there, Birch. I just wanted to make sure you were okay with all those bags."

I blushed at my assumption. "Oh, yeah, it's fine." I turned around to go take a seat, and he finally took his arm out of the door. I apologized to the bus driver as I swiped my pass.

Roughly fifteen minutes later, I was at a stop a few blocks from the house I grew up in. I saw Aaron waiting for me in his usual place a few feet away, leaning against a tree. I often wondered if he waited there all day. It seemed like no matter what time I managed to get on the bus, he was always there waiting for me.

He grabbed the bags from me without solicitation, just as Garrett had. The only difference was that he wrapped me in a big hug after he had them.

"You know, kid, it wouldn't hurt to come see us more often. You don't have to wait for a Gathering. It's not like we're far away." He gave me a stern look, but I knew he wasn't actually mad.

"Sorry, Dad. I'm just super busy with work and school and..." I hesitated, "and friends." Even though my parents were accepting of my friendship with Garrett, I still tried to shield them from just how often I saw him.

"You mean Garrett?"

I was happy to hear that there was no note of disappointment in his voice. "Emma too." I decided it was best not to directly confirm his suspicion.

We walked to the house where my mom was waiting on the porch, excited to see me. Most Nymphs referred to their guides by their names when humans who knew they were related weren't around. I found it easier, and quite natural at this point, to just call them Mom and Dad. Emma thought it was weird, but Owen said he understood why it would be easier.

After catching up for a few minutes and letting them fuss over me for a few minutes more, we finally started preparing for the Gathering. We began bunching together sage, rosemary, and pine needles for the cleansing ritual that would start the Gathering. Shortly after a small handful of bunches were complete, Armeta asked me how Garrett was doing.

"He's okay, I guess." Again, pretending like I didn't see him very often.

"What do you mean, 'you guess?' Don't you work together and live in the same building?" Armeta was always too logical for her own good.

"Well, yeah."

"Then, I imagine you must see him quite frequently," she deduced further.

"Frequently is a strong word." I hoped she would sense my attempt to sidestep the subject and let me do so.

"When was the last time you saw him?" she pressed.

I sighed. I didn't like telling them outright lies. "This morning, actually. I ran into him on my way out of the building."

"Ella," Aaron started.

I had a good idea of what he was going to say. "Don't worry. He didn't see what was in the bags, and even if he had, I could have come up with an explanation. And he doesn't know I was coming here, either. I told him I was volunteering at a women's shelter." I was careful to avoid their gazes so I wouldn't have to see the possible disappointment on their faces.

"Why on Earth did you tell him that? Why not just tell him you were visiting us?" Armeta asked.

Of all the questions she could have asked, of course she asked the one that could shed light on just how often I saw Garrett. On just how close we were.

"Because then he would have wanted to come with me." I avoided looking at them again, instead focusing on the bundle I was tying together.

"There is nothing to be ashamed of in having a human friend, Ella." Aaron's words were comforting, but somehow, I got the feeling he might change his mind if he knew everything I wasn't saying.

"Thanks, but tell that to the Elders. I don't think they share your sentiment."

In fact, I knew they didn't. I found that out firsthand when I was still in elementary school. They had caught wind of my budding friendship with Garrett and made a point to tell me that it was not 'advisable' and that they strongly recommended I terminate any interactions with the human. That was part of why I'd always hidden our closeness from my parents. I didn't want them to get into trouble for my indiscretions.

"Maybe not, but Garrett is a good man. You know we like him, and we know that he watches out for you, which is comforting since you hardly check in with us these days," Armeta teased.

I was happy that Armeta turned the conversation lighthearted. I also found it amusing that she referred to Garrett as a man. I knew he was old enough now to be considered a man, but I had never heard him referred to as such before. It sounded odd, yet appropriate. Maybe that was why he was sporting facial hair now. Maybe he felt it made him look older.

The rest of our conversations stayed light while we finished preparing for the Gathering. Once all the ceremonial items were finished, Armeta helped me get ready. She put about a dozen small braids in my hair, intertwining them with ivy, and I did the same for her. Aaron left us to change into his white cotton oxford shirt and tan capri pants, and we put on our matching white cotton sun dresses.

Once we all had on the appropriate attire, we deposited our ceremonial items into various totes and walked to the nearest bus stop. I was glad we didn't have to dress like the Nymphs of human mythology did. Those outfits were incredibly skimpy and old fashioned looking. That would definitely draw attention. Instead, we looked like we could easily be heading to church or a picnic.

The bus took us to a very remote area, despite the fact that we were only an hour outside of the city. It was very green and lush here, reminiscent of my Birth Forest, however, nowhere near as beautiful. The air was also not as fresh and crisp as where I came from. Regardless, I reveled in the proximity to such dense nature. It was almost as though I was drawing energy from it.

I could swear that the trees turned greener and the flowers brighter as I passed by them. I turned back to smile at my parents who always seemed to walk behind me whenever we got to the Gathering. They were exchanging a meaningful glance, and I felt as though I had intruded on a private, intimate moment.

It was a few miles' walk into the forest before we came to the opening where the Gathering was to occur. I allowed myself to be absorbed in the sounds of nature. The birds chirping, some squirrels bickering in the distance. I thought I could even hear a deer rubbing his antlers against a tree in the distance. I marveled at the way the sun shone through the canopy, lighting up some younger trees' leaves to a brilliant green. The golden light filtered through in an almost heavenly way. I was so wrapped up in my surroundings, I was a little startled when I found people in the clearing. They were Nymphs, of course. The first to arrive at the clearing. Long ago, there had been a magicked barrier put in place in order to keep humans from straying in.

They must not have gotten here much sooner than we had, as they were still placing the food for the feast onto the wooden tables that permanently resided here. They were the most beautiful tables, made from a fallen tree cut vertically down the middle. The tree was left in the most natural state possible, with the bottom of the table being the rounded outside of the trunk, bark still attached. All around the clearing were other fallen trees, dragged into the area to be used as benches. We did not cut down a tree unless we absolutely had to, and not without a ceremony and blessing celebration beforehand.

Armeta and Aaron immediately began placing the cleansing sticks we made on top of the bench logs, spacing them just right, as though they were setting them on individual chairs. I started gathering loose twigs and dry leaves for the fire pit, nodding at the other family as I passed them. In my search for twigs, I made my way to a tree that had been damaged in a lightning storm a few months ago. I happened upon it by accident the first time I saw it and immediately offered it my assistance. Every Gathering since then, I made sure to visit the tree and offer it a little more of my energy to speed up its healing.

When I found it today, I was happy to see it had almost completely healed. I placed my hand upon its bark and felt my energy seep into it. I quickly felt where the most damage was and did my best to send all of my energy to that point.

Once the transfer was done, I removed my hand and watched as some of the bark started growing together at the split. It was almost as though they were stitches bringing two edges of skin together so that the muscles could reconnect and heal back together. When I turned to head back to the clearing with my arms full of kindling, I saw Aaron standing in awe, looking at the tree.

"How long have you been healing this tree?" He finally tore his eyes from the fusing bark to look at me.

I shrugged. "Two or three months, maybe."

"Wow."

I was surprised by his apparent shock. "Yeah, she's a strong tree. It's a little surprising that she isn't a Mother Tree." I'd learned long ago how to tell the difference.

"Strong, indeed." Aaron finally wiped the dumbstruck look off his face and eyed the load I carried. "I came to see if you needed help gathering kindling, but it looks like you have plenty."

When we returned to the clearing, it looked as though everyone had arrived. The table was overflowing with food for the feast, and everyone already had their shoes removed, so as to be in direct contact with Mother Earth.

The Elders were assembled opposite the table, each sitting in an ornately carved chair. These were also made from fallen trees. There were four chairs, made from two different trees. The ones on the outside were made from a pine that was cut into two large stumps and carved into seats, leaving the bark intact wherever possible, including on the entire backside.

The two chairs in the middle were created the same way, however, they were made from oak. These had a slightly more delicate design and were the chairs of the Higher Elders, Ursula and Eugene.

When we were little, we always sat near our guides, but now that we were adults ourselves, Emma and I sat with each other and a few of our other Nymph friends. I looked around the circle and smiled at all the children there. There must have been a dozen of them. There were only a few of them that I didn't recognize, which meant they were most likely newborns.

The pine chair dwelling Elders, Olivia and Ian, lit the fire in the middle of the clearing, and everyone approached it with their cleansing sticks. Once all of the sticks were smoking appropriately, an opening prayer to Goddess Artemis was said by the Elders as the rest of us danced around the fire, waving the smoking sticks through the air in graceful patterns that bathed us all in their aroma.

Once the prayer was over, we simultaneously threw them into the fire, which then began to smoke profusely.

A blessing was said by the High Elders, and we all felt an energy similar to electricity pass from the earth, into our feet, up through our bodies, and back down to the earth.

That had been unnerving for me at my first Gathering. I thought Mother Earth was going to take all my energy, and I wouldn't be able to help any trees. I glanced around at the newborns and saw a range of emotions on their faces. Some looked concerned, as I had, while others looked thrilled and excited, like Emma had.

The Elders proceeded to introduce the newborns and welcome them to the clan. A few families spoke of accomplishments in their neighborhoods, as well as requested help on a few pressing matters of great concern. I volunteered to help Owen's family gather signatures on a petition to stop a developer from cutting down an old growth forest to build another unneeded shopping center.

I saw Emma glare at me as my hand went up, and she promptly raised hers as well. I supposed that meant she hadn't broken up with him yet, and I noticed Arthur eyeing them throughout the night.

Once every family that wanted to had the chance to speak, the High Elders offered a closing blessing. At the end of the blessing, we all stooped down to grab a handful of earth, which we rubbed on each arm, repeating the blessing. As the earth ran across my arms, I could feel a buzz of that same energy that had passed through me in the opening blessing.

I had asked Emma before if she felt it too, and she told me I was imagining it. When I asked my parents, they looked at each other for a few moments while I waited for their response in agony. They assured me that I was probably just feeling a residual effect from the earlier blessing.

With the 'business' out of the way, everyone began mingling, and a queue formed for the food. Never wanting to wait in line, my friends and I had long since decided we should go for a little walk through the forest while the wait died down. About halfway through my junior year, one of them decided we should also add some pot smoking to this walk.

I saw Owen walking with his friend Elijah toward the forest path at the back of the group, just behind Emma. I ran over to join them, and we proceeded into the forest. We had barely cleared the tree line when someone lit the joint.

Strictly speaking, it wasn't looked down on to smoke pot in our community. After all, it came from the earth. But since it was illegal in the human community, we felt it wise to hide it from our guides, even though a lot of them smoked as well.

The joint was passed to me finally, and I took a long drag, knowing how greedy the other smokers were. I held the smoke in my lungs until I felt like either they would burst or I would pass out. Emma started walking backward in front of me as soon as I took my hit. She liked me to blow the smoke in her face so she could get more, so when I could not survive without air any longer, I finally released the smoke slowly, blowing it directly at her.

When I inhaled a breath of fresh air, I felt my mind swirl. I wasn't sure if it was the pot or the lack of oxygen, but suspected it was probably a combination of both. I looked around the forest as the greens became greener, and the browns became warmer.

I felt like I could swim through the golden air and suddenly became aware of my limbs swinging, as though unattached from my body. I could feel energy flowing from the earth beneath my feet, up into my legs, and spreading across my body. This connection was the only way I knew I wasn't floating. I heard someone laugh in the distance. When I realized it was actually Owen, who was right next to me, I cracked up as well. It felt like we had just left when we made it back to the clearing, but there was no longer anyone around the food. We eagerly loaded up the plates that Garrett had helped me carry to the bus.

As I ate the passion fruit that I carefully selected, I thought it must be the best thing I had ever tasted. Then, I ate a chunk of honeydew and decided that it was. Garrett was still on my mind, and I found myself wondering what he would taste like. Would his lips taste like this yummy passion fruit, or would his kiss taste more like honeydew? I doubted it would be either, deciding that he would probably taste like a cigarette.

Before pushing that train of thought completely out of my mind, I quickly invited everyone to go out with me and Garrett that night. Emma seemed a little annoyed, but I knew she wouldn't pass up the opportunity to be around Garrett in a group that he could easily be excluded from.

Of course, I wouldn't let that happen. That was why I invited so many Nymphs. Emma would be so busy socializing with them in an attempt to keep them from talking to Garrett that she wouldn't notice me paying more attention to him than her.

As was customary, the Elders were the first to leave. I was happy that they left a little earlier than usual, but it was still after dark. I wandered over to my parents to tell them I was leaving and found them near the fire, Aaron's arms wrapped around Armeta. They assured me that they would bring home the supplies I had brought, and when we said goodbye, they didn't stand to hug me as they usually would, which I didn't mind.

By the time I made it back to my friends, I noticed that all the families with little ones and teenagers had already left. The adults that remained were all very cozy and seemed to be in their own worlds. I always left before the majority of the adults, but usually not this early.

As we walked the path back to the bus stop, I trailed behind. My friends were carrying on and being loud, and I wanted to enjoy the silence of nature while I still could. It wasn't long before Owen had slowed down enough for me to catch up to him, as he usually did. We walked together in silence, enjoying each other's company. He truly was like a brother to me, and not in the denial sort of way that I considered Garrett to be.

Halfway back, he lit a joint and passed it over to me. I looked at him with surprise, and he just smiled in return. After the first few hits, I felt like I was floating across the forest floor and that with one tiny leap, I could be floating above the trees. With my shoes on I didn't have that energy connection that let me know I was grounded. We were quick to finish smoking it so that we could catch up to our friends before we left the forest.

On the bus, Emma made a pretty prominent display of her and Owen's 'love' for each other. She couldn't keep her hands, or her lips, off him. I assumed it was because she was high. Owen, being a guy, didn't really mind. The rest of us tried not to stare, and luckily, Arthur hadn't joined us. I felt so bad for Owen, knowing that she was leading him on like this with every intention of breaking his heart. I did my best not to think about it, instead focusing on the lights blurring past.

CHAPTER 4

When we finally made it back to campus, everyone went to their respective homes to change. I decided to leave the ivy in my hair and chose a well-worn pair of jeans and a vintage t-shirt to wear with it. Emma and Owen arrived at my door shortly after I was ready. We headed upstairs to Garrett's apartment, and I wished we had a little more pot.

When Garrett opened the door, he wasn't ready yet. I assumed he must have gotten out of the shower rather recently because his hair was slightly damp and he didn't have a shirt on yet. I stood in the doorway like a deer in headlights, admiring his body. I hadn't seen him shirtless in a very long time, and he had toned up quite a bit since then. His abdomen was defined and had more hair than he did the last time I saw him like this. There was a small, unkempt trail of black, slightly curly hair leading from his belly button down to the line of his boxer-briefs that just barely showed above the waistline of his jeans. There was a thinner concentration of hair that covered most of his belly and went part way up his chest. I was surprised that I didn't find the hair appalling, but then I realized that it just furthered his status as a man. When I finally tore my eyes from his physique, I saw him trying to hide a smirk. I had been caught, but being as high as I was, I didn't really care.

He let us in and gave each of us a beer. I watched Garrett out of the corner of my eye as he tried to pick out a shirt. Deciding he was taking too long, I got up to help him.

His apartment was bigger than mine. He didn't like the idea of sleeping in the same room you cook in, so he forked over the extra rent money each month for a one bedroom.

I stumbled into his room and nearly tripped over his shoes. "Jesus!"

He laughed at me and grabbed my waist to steady me. "Easy there, Ella. Did you start without me?"

Instinctually, my hands reached out and grabbed his forearms, providing further support. His skin was cool to the touch. "I haven't had a drop to drink. Honest."

One of his hands reached up to touch the ivy in my hair. I was suddenly very aware of our proximity. "What's going on here?" he asked.

Before I could make something up, I heard Emma behind me. "Yes, what is going on here?"

I shot her a look before turning back to Garrett. I let go of his arms and took a step back, which caused him to let go of my waist. I immediately wished I hadn't taken that step. "Some of the kids at the shelter wanted to play with my hair. They did the same to Emma, but she decided to take it out before being seen in public."

Garrett looked at Emma's hair, and I was glad that the crimps from the braids were still visible, providing evidence for my story.

"Oh, I didn't know Emma was going with you." He looked at me with soft eyes, but I could tell there was a hint of disappointment about our interruption.

For a moment, I got lost in those eyes. They were the most beautiful blue. Not as pale as the sky, but not as bright as the ocean in the tropics, they had a clearness to them like if you put blue-tinted water in a glass and looked through it. And they were bright with life, nearly blindingly so. After a moment's hesitation while I admired his eyes, I finally uttered, ever articulate, "Yeah."

Once again Emma's voice intruded on what should have been a private moment between us. "Just pick a damn shirt, and let's go. I'm losing my buzz, and our friends are already there." She turned to walk away, and I could have sworn I heard her say, "Brother, my ass," on her way back to Owen.

"I thought you were just inviting Emma."

"Well, I figured the more of her friends that were there, the more likely she'd be to leave us alone." I was embarrassed to admit it, but somehow, my filter wasn't working.

"Ella, I think you are probably the smartest person I know." He finally chose a dark green shirt, and we headed to the bar.

While on the way there, Garrett tried to hold my hand. Somewhere in my mind, I knew I shouldn't let him, but instead of listening to that far away voice, I concentrated on how my hand felt tingly in his.

Tracy and Felicia were waiting for us outside the bar, and I noticed Tracy giving me an evil glare. A giggle involuntarily escaped my lips, which then made me laugh harder. Owen, having shared that extra joint with me, laughed as well, even though he had no idea what I was laughing about. Garrett just looked at us like we were crazy.

Inside, we found our Nymph friends and joined them. As I suspected, Emma did everything she could to ignore Garrett, and Tracy did all she could to attract his attention. We sat at a long table, which made it so that many conversations were happening at once. I was sitting across from Garrett with Tracy on his left. It suited me just fine because I always felt it was easier to converse with someone if you weren't right next to them.

I watched Tracy flirt with Garrett, and it really did look like Garrett had no idea she was into him. I felt bad for her. She was a pretty girl, but she decided to have a thing for the one guy too dense to realize he was being flirted with. She was resting her hand on his forearm, leaning her whole body toward him.

When Garrett caught me watching their exchange, he was quick to include me. "What's your favorite class, Ella?"

I smiled bigger than I probably should have. "Mythology." I looked over at Tracy and saw her expression change from annoyance to anxiety. I thought I'd have a little fun with her, so I leaned forward and grabbed a loose hair from her shirt. "Oh, Tracy, you have a hair on your shirt. Let me get that." Instead of letting it go, I made it look like I put it into my pocket.

Garrett gave me a stern look, but it softened when I flashed him a sheepish smile.

I picked up my beer bottle to cheer and said, "To mythology."

Almost the entire table, most being Nymphs, yelled out, "Here, here," in response. Tracy left shortly after that, dragging Felicia with her. I felt kind of bad, imagining her freaked out all night that I would use that hair to create a Voodoo doll, but I quickly let the thought go. I'd had quite a few beers at this point, and they were really intensifying my already intense high.

Garrett started telling me about his day, and I noticed how velvety his voice was. It felt as though it could wrap me up and keep me warm. His blue eyes dazzled in the dim light, and his blondish brown facial hair caught that same light and became golden brown. I pulled my foot out of my shoe and playfully slid it up his leg, stopping just above his knee and watched his eyes widen.

"Whoa there, Ella. What are you doing?"

"Just having some fun." I took another drink from my beer bottle, surprised to find it empty afterward. I set it down next to its three other friends.

"That kind of fun can get dangerous," he said, but I could see a fire light in his eyes.

"I like danger. Don't you?" I slid my foot a little higher.

"You know I do."

I felt his hand on my ankle, pulling my foot higher still. I laughed and pulled it out of his hand.

"Now that's just not fair," he complained.

Finally, the waitress came by, and we each ordered another beer. My fifth and his sixth.

"And what are you gonna do about it?" I asked once she walked away. "You're way over there. I don't think I have anything to worry about."

"I guess I'll just have to fix that then."

I didn't understand what he meant until he got up and walked around the table, sitting in the empty seat next to me.

"You sure you like danger?" he asked, leaning slightly closer to me.

The waitress brought us our new beers, and we each took a long swig.

I put the bottle back down and said, "You know I do."

He leaned even closer and put his hand on my thigh, just above my knee.

"Is that all you got?" I saw his hand-on-the-leg and raised him one higher up, placing my hand halfway between his knee and hip. He raised an eyebrow and slid his hand closer to my hip, his fingers gripping the inside of my thigh.

We were suddenly very close together. I glanced down at his lips. They looked soft and tender. I remembered my earlier question. *Passion fruit or honey dew?* I looked back at his eyes. He leaned closer still.

"This is a very dangerous game," he noted.

"Yes, very dangerous," I agreed. Though it didn't seem possible, we leaned even closer together. Our lips were almost touching. *Passion fruit or honey dew?* "It's probably a bad idea." I could almost feel my lips brushing against his as I spoke.

"Definitely, very bad." He hesitated, his lips a breath away from touching mine. "Maybe we should go back to my place and sort this out."

"Yeah, maybe," I agreed and closed my eyes. I felt as though my lips were trembling and my knees wobbling.

Just as I started closing the tiny gap between us and he began running his hand even farther up my thigh, I was torn back to reality by someone calling out my name. I very suddenly became aware of his hand. And my hand. I was so high on his thigh, I knew I was mere centimeters away from touching him. I realized that our legs were intertwined, and our entire upper bodies leaned toward each other as though we wouldn't be able to breathe if we were any farther apart.

I immediately sat straight up and removed my hand. Garrett followed suit, then took a large drink from his beer. I turned my head in the direction that I heard my name called and found Emma's face, a few seats away, crying. I was happy to see that her own drama seemed to have made her blind to what almost happened between me and Garrett. I could only hope that it really did blind her and that she wasn't just ignoring it for now, having decided that her crisis was more important.

"Oh my God, Emma, what's wrong?"

Out of the corner of my eye, I saw Garrett run one of his hands through his hair in what I could only guess was frustration. My thigh still tingled where his hand had been and I idly wondered if his did too.

"I broke up with Owen!"

Poor Owen. "That's what you wanted, remember?" I glanced around the room, trying to find him. If Emma was this broken up about it, I couldn't even imagine how miserable he must be, but he was nowhere to be seen.

"I know, but it was horrible. He acted like it was no big deal and he didn't care."

My eyes rolled without my permission. I began to suspect that she did notice what was happening between me and Garrett and that was why she was making this so much more dramatic than it was. I was angry with her at the time for stopping me before I got a chance to taste Garrett's kiss, for not waiting even ten seconds to interrupt with her drama, but I knew I would be grateful for it later.

"He probably just didn't want you to feel bad. I'll bet that's why he left. So that he could be upset about it without you seeing."

Emma sniffled. "Yeah, you're probably right. I'm just a mess. Can I stay at your place tonight? I don't want to deal with my roommate." Emma's eyes glanced over at Garrett as she asked.

Emma's roommate was a human, which I had always thought was odd since she looked down on them. I supposed she only put up with it because it meant she didn't have to pay as high of rent for her more spacious apartment right next to campus.

Garrett sighed.

"Of course you can stay over, Emma. It'll be like old times. We haven't had a slumber party in ages!" I did my best to sound enthused.

With Emma dragging the mood down, I quickly paid my tab and said goodbye to the rest of our Nymph friends so that I could get her home. Garrett insisted on walking us there. He tried to hold my hand while we were walking, but I wouldn't let him. I had sobered up enough to realize what a bad idea it would be, especially in front of Emma.

He walked us all the way to my apartment door, and once Emma was inside, he finally decided to speak. "If it gets too crowded in there, you can always come stay with me." His smile didn't reach his eyes, and I knew he knew I would refuse.

"Thanks, Garrett, for everything. But we both know that isn't a good idea." Trying to ease the tension, I quickly added, "After all, Emma can't be trusted alone."

He smiled again, but it was smaller this time. He said goodnight and kissed my forehead before heading to the stairway and up to his apartment.

I felt absolutely exhausted by the time we changed into pajamas. All I wanted to do was curl up under my covers and fall asleep. Unfortunately, my house guest wanted to gab all night. I still curled up under my covers, but sleep could not find me. Instead, I listened the best I could, nodded where appropriate, and offered up an 'uh-huh' every now and then.

She talked about Owen and Arthur and the Gathering. She went on and on about how she couldn't wait to sit with Arthur at the next Gathering and how she hoped it wouldn't be awkward because of Owen. Somehow, I didn't believe her on that last bit.

My eyes were drooping closed by the time she decided to bring up my encounter with Garrett. "Oh. My. God. Ella! What was going on with you and Garrett tonight?!"

I was so glad I was tired enough to get out of this conversation. "Absolutely nothing. Just a couple of drunk friends goofing around. I'm really tired, Emma, so I'm going to sleep now." What I really meant was that *we* were going to sleep now, seeing as it would be nearly impossible for one person to sleep and one to stay awake in a studio apartment.

I was abrupt about it, but sometimes, that was the best way to snap Emma out of her self-absorption. Within minutes of being bathed in silence, I was out like a light.

CHAPTER 5

I woke quite early the next day and was not at all surprised to find Emma still sleeping. It looked like a beautiful day outside, so I decided that I would head to the community garden that was sponsored by the university.

The seeds and equipment were donated from local businesses, and the labor was volunteered by students, mostly agriculture and biology majors, as could be expected since the garden was on campus grounds. I tended an eight foot by four foot raised bed where I grew a variety of vegetables for local food banks.

When I got there, I was surprised to find another person up so early. He was working on the bed across from mine. As I approached, I noticed a shift in his composure. My presence seemed to make him shy. He gave me a quick smile but avoided eye contact. He fumbled with tools that he had been using just fine before he saw me and suddenly developed an interest in smoothing his already smooth hair.

I smiled and said hello as I walked past, causing him to almost drop the hand rake he was using. I kneeled on the ground in front of my cucumbers and began weeding. Every time I glanced up, I looked over at my neighbor. He was handsome in a not-so-obvious way. Not ruggedly handsome like Garrett and not movie-star cute like Owen, this guy was the type that wouldn't attract a double take, but if someone had taken the time, they would notice him. He had coarse looking dark blonde hair that he wore a little too long. My guess was that he did so in order to distract from his large almond shaped eyes. I couldn't see their color from where I sat, but I could tell there was some pain behind them.

During one of my observations, he tucked some of his hair that was getting in his line of sight behind his ear. He looked over at me when he did this, and I was caught. I tried to offer him a friendly smile, but he averted his eyes much too quickly.

I had made it through most of my garden at this point and now had to move to a very close proximity to him. He was tending to some tomato plants. In an effort at friendliness, I tried to engage him in conversation. "Are those cherry tomatoes or grape?"

He seemed startled by the sound of my voice, but he glanced up very briefly before returning to his work and mumbled his response, "Grape." His voice was hoarse, as though he hadn't spoken in some time.

"You're going to want to pick those very soon then. If you let them go much longer, they'll go bad right there on the vine."

He nodded in acknowledgement.

When he didn't offer any other response, I tried again. "I'm surprised I haven't seen you out here before." I glanced at the sign at the edge of his garden that indicated who was responsible for tending it. I half expected it to say Chess Club, what with his social anxiety. "Did you just recently join the Future Farmers of America?"

My question seemed to confuse him. He recovered rather quickly, though. "Uh, no, I just, um, usually come out here at, uh, at nighttime only."

I smiled to myself, happy that he offered more than just a yes or no. "I'm Ella, by the way." I brushed off my hands and offered one to him.

He awkwardly shook it. "Austin."

For a moment, I thought that was all he would say, but courage seemed to suddenly build in him, and he offered a compliment.

"Your garden is amazing. Best one here."

I glanced around at all twelve plots. While all were kept presentable, most didn't look to be yielding very much produce. My plants were bigger and heartier looking than all of them. I frowned a little. I had never noticed before. I looked back at Austin and gave a small smile. "Thanks. I guess my dirt has a good pH balance."

"I'll bet it's more than that. What's your real secret?" A slightly devilish smile spread across his face, surprising me a little.

"No secret, really. I guess I just have a green thumb. Years of gardening can do that."

His smile faded, and he returned to his work. We didn't say anything else after that, and as soon as I was finished tending my vegetables, I headed back home. Naturally, Emma was still lying in my bed, so I politely kicked her out, promising to call her later. Once she was gone, I called Owen. I still hadn't been able to talk to him post break up.

"Oh, hey, Ella." He sounded oddly chipper.

"Hi. I heard about you and Emma. I'm so sorry."

"Oh, that?"

I was slightly taken aback. He said it dismissively rather than the depressed version I had expected. "Yeah, that. You doing okay?"

He laughed. "I'm fine, Ella. Quit worrying."

"I don't understand. I thought you loved her, but you sound almost happy about breaking up." I felt as though I missed something.

"Whoa, I wouldn't say 'happy.' It's more like I know it's only temporary," he explained.

"Temporary how?" Now I felt really thick. I seemed to have missed something huge.

"Come on, Ella. You, of all people, know how she is. She just saw something shiny and got distracted. She'll be back in no time." I always admired the inherent confidence Owen had, but this seemed extreme.

"Something shiny? What, like a light bulb?"

He laughed again. "Not literally, you weirdo. A guy. She met some guy, and he probably flirted with her, and she decided she wanted something new and exciting. His novelty will wear off, and she'll be back in no time at all."

Huh. I hadn't thought of it that way, but it did sound like classic Emma. "And you're okay with that?"

"Well, of course I wish she wouldn't get distracted, but that's just how she is, and I can't change her."

I considered this. "I don't know. If it were me and..." I paused, realizing I had been about to say me and Garrett. Instead, I sidestepped that mess and tried again. "If it were me, and my boyfriend broke up with me to run off with some other girl, I don't think I could be so forgiving."

"Ah yes, well, you and Garrett don't count." I could hear the stupid smirk he was undoubtedly wearing in his voice.

"Me and Garrett? What are you talking about? What does he have to do with this?"

"Because if you did have a boyfriend, it would be Garrett—and don't deny that he came to mind just then—and you two don't count."

I sighed. "Okay, fine. For argument's sake, we'll go with that. But just why wouldn't we count?"

"Man, I have to spell everything out for you today. You don't count because you guys have been in love with each other since forever."

I immediately got defensive. "We have not!"

"Okay, you're right. Maybe not forever, but at least since kindergarten."

"That's just ridiculous, Owen."

"Are you really going to sit there and tell me you don't love him?"

"Sure, I love him. He's like a brother to me."

"No, Ella, *I'm* like a brother to you. You two are *in* love."

"You're wrong," I insisted.

"Okay, fine. Maybe you don't feel that way about him, which I don't believe for a second. But he is definitely in love with you. He has been for quite a while."

My body betrayed me, allowing my heart to skip a beat at that bit of information. "There's no way. He is not!" My cheeks flushed at the immaturity I was showing. I knew I sounded like I was in high school.

"Jesus, Ella, can you really not see it?"

"See what?"

"How much he loves you. No matter where we are or what we're doing, he keeps his proximity close to you. He watches you when you talk; he smiles when you do any of the weird things you do. His face lights up when you enter the room. Hell, he's even recycling and being environmentally conscious for you!"

"What weird things?" It made me self-conscious to think I was doing strange things in public.

"Really? All that and the thing you're most concerned about are your weird mannerisms?" He sounded exasperated.

"Well, yeah! What if I'm doing something, I don't know, Nymphish?"

He laughed hysterically. "I don't think that you blowing into your straw before putting it in your drink screams Nymph."

"Hey! I just want to make sure none of the wrapper stuck to the straw!" Seriously. What was weird about that?

"Stuck to the inside?" His voice held a tone of mockery.

"Whatever, Owen. I don't want to talk about me. I called to see how you were doing."

"Peachy keen. Thanks."

"Good. Can you come by tomorrow when I get home from work and help me harvest the garden?"

"Why don't you get Garrett to help you? You two seemed pretty cozy at the bar last night."

Of course Owen saw that. "Damn it, Owen. I told you we aren't talking about that. Can you help or not?"

"Sure. Geez. Don't get your panties in a bunch."

"Great," I said, kind of pointedly. "And for the record, as my self-proclaimed 'brother,' you shouldn't be thinking about the state of my panties!"

He started laughing at me again, and I hung up on him. Now that I was all worked up, I couldn't just sit still. I needed to do something. Anything. My apartment was already rather tidy, so I decided to go buy my books for the fall semester. It was starting the middle of next week, and I had yet to take care of any of my shopping because I was busy finishing my summer semester.

Unfortunately, book buying didn't take very long, and I still had pent up energy. Rather than let it go to waste, I decided to spend the rest of the day at my favorite local food bank, packaging boxes to be picked up by families in need. It was decent physical labor and thought provoking enough to distract me from my frustration with Owen. By the time I arrived back home, I was so tired and my feet ached so badly that I crashed immediately.

I was awoken suddenly by the annoying beeping of my alarm. I had been dreaming about my Mother Tree in the Smoky Mountains. She was just as I remembered her, full of warmth and serenity, but the version of me with her looked how I do now. My dream self also had all of my memories. I was looking around the forest in wonder, watching the leaves blowing in the wind and listening to them rustle. It was the most beautiful sound I had ever heard. Better than even the best orchestra. More calming than the sound of waves breaking against a sandy beach. I never wanted to leave this place, just like I hadn't when Aaron and Armeta had retrieved me.

I watched as my dream self finally tore her gaze from the surrounding scenery and focused on my Mother Tree. I approached her slowly while raising my arm in anticipation of placing my palm on her beautiful bark. She was a great old black gum tree that stood taller than most of her neighbors. She filtered the light beautifully through her canopy, causing beams of golden light to exist as though they were spotlights. As my hand extended to a spotlight, I felt the warmth of the sun all the way to my core. No, I never wanted to leave her again.

Finally, my dream self reached her destination, just inches from my Mother Tree's trunk. In what seemed like slow motion, she leaned forward, reaching out her hand until it made contact with the bark. Several things happened at once when my dream self's palm rested flat against her bark.

First, there was a warm sense of welcoming. She remembered me. She knew I was hers, and she still loved me. It was a very sweet feeling to know she had missed me as I had missed her.

Within seconds of processing this, I also picked up on something else. Something foreboding. It was like she wanted to warn me. And apologize to me. She felt that she had betrayed me, but I had no idea why. I didn't even know how it was possible to be betrayed by a tree, Mother Tree or otherwise. There was such disappointment there, disappointment in herself. I felt the need to break contact with her so as to not have to feel such powerful negative emotions.

Instead, I decided that I could maybe help. After all, I was a Nymph. It was in my very nature to heal trees. How could I not try to heal my Mother Tree? Sure, she didn't have a physical injury, but that didn't make it any less tangible.

I sent her as much energy as I could, along with a sentiment of forgiveness, though I had no idea what I was forgiving. I just knew that I didn't want her in pain. And certainly not pain associated with me. My dream self removed her hand and took a step back. That was when I noticed that my Mother Tree had a large gash in her trunk. There was dried sap at the bottom of the gash where she had bled.

It wasn't obvious enough to notice before, but now that it was healing thanks to my energy, it stood out like a beacon. I touched the spot as it healed, more out of curiosity than anything else. I hadn't expected anything to come of it since I had already offered my energy and she was healing.

I was surprised and disoriented when I saw a flash of a knife digging into her bark. It was slow and deliberate, as though the knife's wielder had known it would cause her pain. I felt her fear and her pain. Just as I removed my hand from her in shock, my alarm woke me up.

Upon waking, I felt like I hadn't slept at all. Maybe not even for a few days. It was as though the energy transfer had really taken place on top of having a restless night. Some depression lingered from the dream, and with it, a hint of disgust. How anyone could deliberately harm a Mother Tree was beyond me.

I felt so angry about it that it took a while for me to calm down, reassuring myself that it was only a dream. I still couldn't get the image of that hand digging the knife into her bark and dragging it down ever so slowly. I shivered at the thought. I decided I'd have to have a pilgrimage of some sort and visit her. It wasn't a common thing for a Nymph to do, but it wasn't unheard of. But for now, I had to get to work.

It would be the first time I had seen Garrett since we pushed the envelope at the bar. I wasn't looking forward to the awkwardness that would surely pass between us, but I hoped that pretending as though nothing had happened would suffice to brush that awkwardness away.

Boy, was I wrong. I was the first one to arrive, as per usual. I turned on the lights and opened the windows to let in a fresh breeze. Others didn't start filtering in until I started a pot of coffee, as though they were being drawn to it by some invisible, gravitational pull.

Garrett showed up about ten minutes late, but I didn't call him out on it. He was a co-founder, even if he didn't like to think so, and I didn't want to point out his tardiness amongst the ranks. Better to let them assume he had planned on coming in late and that I had known about said plan. I also didn't want to rock the boat, seeing as how I was sure it was already in rough waters.

My assumption was confirmed as the morning progressed. Normally, he would talk to me almost as soon as he came in, but today, he ignored me. It was as though I wasn't even in the room. I felt certain that this proved Owen wrong, but it wasn't exactly something I felt like gloating about.

I eventually had to seek him out so that we could talk about the afternoon staff meeting. I found him in the copy room, arranging the reams of recycled paper by color. Surely, it wasn't something that needed to be done, and it definitely wasn't something that needed to be done by him.

"Hey," I started tentatively.

"Oh, hey, Ella." He offered a small smile, but the twinkle was missing from his unfairly gorgeous eyes.

"I was wondering if you had anything you wanted to bring up in this afternoon's meeting?"

"Nope."

I let out an uncomfortable laugh. "You don't even know what I plan on talking about. How could you possibly know there's nothing you want to add?"

He studied me for a moment, and I noticed how his eyes looked like storm clouds. I could swear they were actually swirling like storm clouds. Different shades of blue from his typical clear and icy to brilliantly blinding.

"Okay, shoot.," he said. "What do you plan on talking about?"

"Well, I wanted to remind everyone about the Relay for Life event that we're sponsoring and get volunteers to set up recycle bins for it. Then, I thought I'd take ideas for a team building company outing. And there's this petition that Owen told me about that..." I trailed off as I watched his face slowly form a smile. It appeared more animated than it was, thanks to his thickening facial hair. After standing there in awe at the perfection of it, I finally looked up to his eyes. His twinkle was back, and it made me smile in return. "What?" I asked, suddenly self-conscious that I was doing one of those weird mannerisms that Owen mentioned.

"I just can't stay mad at you. It's impossible."

"Mad? At me? Why were you mad?"

"You're kidding, right? That's a joke? Sometimes, it's hard to tell with your twisted sense of humor."

"No joke." I hadn't expected him to be mad at me. I just thought he'd feel awkward too. We came way too close to crossing the line. It was the kind of thing close friends could have a hard time coming back from.

"Did you black out? After the bar? Did you wake up with no memory of what had transpired the night before?"

"You know I never black out."

"Did you go under hypnosis to forget then?"

"No, I woke up and went to tend my garden," I answered before realizing he was just mocking me. Before he had a chance to make fun of me, I asked, "Why were you mad?"

He sighed and half sat on the table by the mail sorter. "You're such a fucking tease, Ella."

I stared at him, waiting for more. Waiting for enough to make his anger make sense.

Finally, he continued, "You know how I feel about you, and you just use me for your entertainment and throw it in my face."

"I know we're good friends, and we almost crossed the line. I'm sorry about that. I don't know what I would do if I messed up our friendship, but I don't see how I threw that in your face. I don't understand how that makes me a tease."

"So much for being pretty *and* smart," he mumbled to himself. "You know exactly what I mean. Unless you're in some crazy world of super denial."

My brow furrowed in concentration. "We got drunk and got a little flirty."

"We're always a little flirty," Garrett retorted. "And I dare say, that was a bit more than a little."

"Exactly my point!" I went over to close the door to make sure we had privacy. "We were so close to crossing a line because we got too drunk! We could have ruined our friendship. I thought today would just be awkward because of that. I didn't expect you to be mad!" I was exasperated. He made no sense.

"I can't believe you don't already know this, but for the sake of, I don't know, the sake of you not being able to play dumb anymore, I guess I have to spell it out."

"Please do. Spell it out. Because I have no idea what you're talking about."

"Ella, maybe I *wanted* to cross that line." He leaned toward me. "Maybe I'm sick of just being friends. The line is so damned fuzzy, it's hard to see it anymore anyway. You and I, we have this connection, this heat. I've never experienced that with anyone else."

I stood there in shock, mouth agape like an imbecile. Garrett took a step toward me.

"Ella, you must know how I feel about you. You have to have realized that I, that I lo—"

"No. You don't mean that. Not any of it. We can't. You know we can't. We've already had this conversation. It wouldn't work. We're too good of friends, and it isn't worth the risk."

"No, *you* decided those things, and it has been years. I get if you were afraid then. We were young and inexperienced and naïve. But you can't hide behind those flimsy excuses anymore. I let you get away with it then because I didn't know any better. But I'm not going to let you dismiss it this time."

I thought about the conversation we'd had back in high school. We were sophomores, and he asked me to go ice skating with him. I hadn't realized he meant it as a date, but he did, and he acted as though it was one.

He was a good skater, and I was shaky at best. I had thought it necessitated his holding my hand, but actually, he chose to hold it because it was what you do on a date.

After a fall that hurt my knee, he rolled up my jeans to make sure I hadn't torn any skin. Luckily, it was only a red splotch, which he kissed, and I felt a warmth spread through my body. His lips were so soft and warm. They made me forget I was sitting on cold, hard ice. He met my eyes and started leaning in to kiss me on the lips. I promptly grabbed hold of the boards and lifted myself up, uneasily.

"Hey, where are you going?" he had asked me.

"You know what they say, if you don't get back up on the horse right away, you never will."

"But we're not horseback riding," he teased.

I started to skate away, and he caught up ridiculously fast and started skating backwards in front of me. "Show off." He smiled his twinkly eye smile, and I averted my eyes. "I'm actually pretty cold. We should probably just go." I dared a glance back up just in time to see his smile falter.

"Oh, okay," he said before escorting me off the ice.

It started to snow while we were changing into our sneakers, and I felt awful. I hadn't realized how much I had grown to care about Garrett until he almost kissed me, and I realized that I wanted him to. I also knew we couldn't. The Nymph community didn't appreciate my friendship with a human. They most certainly wouldn't tolerate a romantic relationship.

We walked through the snowfall to the bus stop together in silence. While we were waiting, the silence turned deafening. When I couldn't take it anymore, I finally spoke up.

"Hey, thanks. I had a lot of fun. Even if I did suck."

He acted as though he hadn't even heard me. Instead, he spoke what had been on his mind. "Ella, if I made you uncomfortable, I'm sorry. I thought you knew I meant this as a date."

"Garrett..." I started. I had to look away from his eyes in order to finish. "We just can't, okay? We can't date."

The snow started coming down harder, and I was anxious for the bus to arrive.

"Why not?" He sounded defeated and I felt terrible. It was one of the few times I had wished I were human, just to simplify my life.

My response to his question had been all of the lame excuses he was now telling me that I couldn't hide behind. I forced myself back to the present, and with no excuses left to give, I just told him as much of the truth as I could, which wasn't much.

"We can't be together. I'm sorry, but we can't. We... are too different. It just isn't possible, and that's all there is to it. I really can't explain it. You just have to trust me. There's too much at stake."

The anger returned to his face. "That's bullshit, and you know it."

I shivered, suddenly feeling cold, and felt a pain in my chest as I watched him walk away.

The rest of the day went by just as slowly as the morning. Even the meeting seemed to drag on. Garrett only spoke as much as he had to and avoided eye contact with me whenever possible. The few times he did glance my way, there was an intense glint in his eyes, but I couldn't identify the emotion behind it.

CHAPTER 6

By the time I headed home, I had forgotten about my plans with Owen until I bumped into him on the sidewalk during my short commute—work was literally at the end of the block. I ran upstairs and rushed to change and get ready for working in the garden. I grabbed my baskets to collect the vegetables in and headed back downstairs. We crossed the street and headed down the footpath that would lead us to the community garden.

Owen finally spoke when we were a little ways down the path. "How was work?"

"Fine, I guess. How was your day?"

"Did Garrett talk to you about what happened?" He asked the question as though he already knew the answer.

"Nothing actually happened. What would make you think he'd want to talk about a non-event?"

"I wouldn't call Saturday night a non-event. And I'm sure it's been eating at him for the last two days. Logic dictates that he'd bring it up." After I didn't respond, he added, "So, what'd he say?"

Yes, he definitely knew something. "I think you know exactly what he said, and damn it, Owen, if you put those ideas in his head, I'm going to kill you."

We arrived at the garden, and I noticed Austin was there, tending the same garden as before. He offered a small smile, and I waved.

"I didn't put any ideas in anyone's head."

"Owen," I started.

"Hey, he called me!" Owen explained.

"And what did he tell you?" I knew that Garrett liked Owen, but I was a little surprised that he called him. I knew they sometimes talked on their own and even had hung out a few times, but it seemed odd to me that he didn't confide in one of his human friends.

"You know, guy stuff."

"Really? That's all I get? 'Guy stuff?'"

"Yup. That's all I can say. Guy stuff."

"Okay, fine," I conceded. "What did you tell him about this situation?"

"I just told him that you're oblivious and that you're not as smart as you like people to think."

"Owen!"

"Well, it's true—when it comes to this stuff."

Slightly angry from his insult, I started picking the green beans a little more roughly than I needed to. "He's the oblivious one. He doesn't even realize how much Tracy likes him. He should ask her out, but he's too 'dumb' to notice how she sees him."

The peppers that Owen had been placing in the basket slipped out of his hand as he erupted with laughter.

"What the hell is so funny?" I demanded.

"Hello, Pot. I'd like to introduce you to Kettle."

I rolled my eyes at his lack of originality. "I've already told you to get your eyes checked. You're seeing things when it comes to him and me. And before you say that is just more proof of my blindness, I am not blind! I've seen how Elijah looks at me. I know he likes me."

"Yeah, Elijah does like you, but so does Garrett. I dare say much more than Elijah does."

I sighed. "What makes you so sure?"

"Because, Ella, he told me when he called yesterday. He had thought that he'd made himself perfectly clear over the years, and on Saturday, he thought you had finally gotten the message."

"And so you put ideas in his head about us? Owen, he almost dropped the L word."

"I didn't put anything in his head. I just told him that he had to tell you straight up how he feels. And that you honestly didn't know."

I started in on the peas and thought how best to word what I had to say next. "But don't you see, Owen? That in and of itself is an idea you've put in his head. We can never be together. He's a human and I'm a..." I paused and looked around. Austin was harvesting his garden on the opposite side of his plot. I looked back to Owen. "And I'm a Nymph. It won't work. It can't. It's forbidden," I finished more quietly.

Owen moved on to the cucumbers with a sigh. "It's not actually forbidden. And your guides really like him, I like him—"

"Emma hates him. And it is practically forbidden, even if not literally." I couldn't allow myself the wiggle room of technicality. I knew if Garrett and I started dating, it would be all the harder to hide my true identity from him. It would drive a wedge between us, and there might not be a way to come back from that. I couldn't live with that risk, no matter how much I might want to be with him.

"Emma is just jealous. She's not used to having to share you. Before, when you two were in separate schools, she never had to interact with you and Garrett together. She still didn't like him just because she knew he was a big part of your life. Then, when we were all in high school together, her jealousy increased ten-fold."

I started to protest but had no idea what to say. He was frustratingly making sense.

"You know how our kind can be, Ella," he continued. "Under the right circumstances, the jealousy can be crippling."

He was right, of course. I hadn't seen it happen too often because we usually made a conscious effort to keep it in check, but I had seen jealousy split people apart. When we were little, a big scandal broke out because one of the men in our clan started spending a lot of time with a woman who wasn't his partner. When his partner caught wind of it, she nearly killed the man, and the supposed mistress.

They had both denied getting involved, insisting they were just close friends, but the damage was done. The man and mistress moved to avoid ridicule, and the woman ran off, never to be heard from again. The rumor was that she took to living in the forest, so as to never get involved with anyone again. I was starting to think she had the right idea.

I was about to tell him that he was crazy. That Emma would never let something so petty get between us, but before I could get anything out, Austin approached.

"Hey, Ella."

"Oh, hi, Austin. I've bumped into you twice in one week. You're not stalking me, are you?" I teased.

He looked a little embarrassed, and I remembered his shyness. When he didn't respond, I quickly changed the subject.

"Austin, this is Owen." I gestured to Owen. "And Owen, this is Austin. He's a Future Farmer of America."

"Nice to meet you," Owen said, as he extended his hand.

Austin took it very briefly and mumbled, "Yeah, you too."

"I see you took my advice and harvested." I looked ·down at his basket. His vegetables were sparse compared to mine.

"Uh, yeah. The other guys got most of it, but I came by to grab any stragglers."

"That's cool. Hey, do you want to—"

"I gotta go," Austin said. "It was good to see you again."

"Uh, okay, bye," I said, as he scurried away.

"Interesting guy," Owen commented.

"Yeah, he's pretty shy."

"And pretty weird."

"Be nice, Owen."

"Yes, Mommy."

I playfully smacked him in the stomach before bending down to pick up one of my baskets. They were full of a colorful variety of produce that would certainly make the food bank happy. Owen picked up the two remaining baskets, and we set off on our journey to the food bank.

It was quite a haul when compared to the proximity of my apartment, but it was still within comfortable walking distance. We chose the path that would pass us by the museum because it was more scenic. The museum itself had beautiful architecture and lined its sidewalk with an abundance of flowers and other plant life.

Owen and I exchanged a glance of contentment as we passed through this mini park. I half expected him to produce a joint out of thin air, which I wouldn't have objected to. I was so stressed out about everything with Garrett that I wanted something to help me wind down. Alas, he was not a magician, and no joint materialized in front of us.

I spent the rest of my week trying my best to stay out of Garrett's way. While I knew I couldn't avoid him completely, I figured giving him as much space as possible would help. The last time we had a fight this bad was during our senior year. He started dating one of the goth chicks in school, and she didn't 'appreciate' our friendship. I told him it was bullshit, and he got mad at me. Either way, his girlfriend got her way. We didn't speak for months.

Thankfully, this time, he didn't stay mad as long. I noticed him slowly returning to normal, offering up a smile here or a joke there. Finally, I ran into him at the café, and I discovered that our little rift was over.

We had a coffee together, and he asked me when I'd be going to the laundry mat next door to our apartment building. I knew this meant that all was forgiven, if not forgotten, because we usually did our laundry together so we could entertain each other while waiting for the slow machines to work their magic. As it happened, the fall semester was starting the next day, and I knew I had to get as much laundry done as possible while I still had some semblance of free time.

"I'm actually going tonight. Should I expect company?" I asked.

"Ooh. Man. I can't tonight. I wish you were going tomorrow."

A nervous laugh escaped my lips, though I didn't know why I was nervous. "What's tonight? You got a hot date or something?"

"As a matter of fact, I do. Her name is Bridget, and she works—what am I doing? You don't want to hear about this."

My insides turned over before folding themselves up into an origami dragon that could breathe white hot fire. Or at least, that's what it felt like. "What are you talking about? Why wouldn't I want to hear about this? What does she do?"

Garrett sighed, and for a fraction of an instant, it looked like his face fell slightly. "I was just going to say that she works at this coffee shop I go to sometimes. She flirts with me every time I see her, but I always just play dumb."

"Why? What changed?"

"What do you mean?"

"Why ask her out now? If you've known all this time that she likes you, why are you just now asking her out?"

Garrett shifted his feet and looked down briefly. "I don't know. I guess I just thought I haven't dated anyone in a while. Seemed like a good time to get back in the game."

I downed the rest of my coffee in one gulp. "Well, good for you. And anyway, school starts tomorrow, so I have to do laundry tonight. Have fun on your date. We'll catch up later," I promised before hightailing it out the door.

Once I got home, I immediately started cleaning up and gathering any laundry that managed to evade the confines of the hamper. After finding a pair of purple socks that somehow made it under the couch, I dumped the contents of my hamper into a giant bag, which I then stuffed into a laundry basket, and headed to the laundry mat next door.

It was a small facility with just a few machines, and most of them were out of order. Halfway through my second load, I called my parents. Armeta answered. "Hello?"

"Hey, Mom, what's going on?"

"Oh, Ella, I'm so glad you called! I was just working on your birthday present."

I smiled to myself. Even though my parents were there the day my Mother Tree released me from her branches, my actual birthday, as is true for all Nymphs, was the day I first began sprouting from her.

"Yeah? It's a bit early... What is it?" I responded, knowing full well she wouldn't tell me.

"You know, the usual. A nuclear power plant model, complete with radioactive waste. Had to get an early start. It takes time to make something so complex."

I laughed. She always offered up the most absurd answer when someone asked her something she didn't want to answer. "Is Dad around?"

"Aaron is out in the garden. Did you need him for something?"

"No, not particularly. Just being nosy. What should I bring to the Gathering this week?"

"I'm glad you asked. We just heard that Olga isn't going to be there this time, so we need someone who can bake to bring some cookies."

I laughed again. "Mom, anyone can bake."

"If you say so, but your cookies are the best I've ever tasted."

"Okay, fine. I'll make them. But I'm coming to your house to do it. There just isn't enough room at my place to make that many."

"Oh, that would be wonderful! And I'm going to pretend you're going to do it here because you miss us and not because it's more convenient," she teased.

"Of course I miss you guys! I don't get over there enough, and now that the new semester is starting it's going to be even harder to find time." It made me sad to think about how little I managed to see them. When I was growing up, it seemed like we were always outside together, whether it was in the garden working or just playing in the yard. I used to get into trouble all the time because I thought it was hilarious to make everything grow three sizes too big, including the grass.

"Ella, don't you spread yourself too thin. You need to keep your strength up to be able to fulfill all your duties."

"I know, I know." That was so like Armeta, always the worrier. ""Look, Mom, I have to go. My dryer is finished. But I'll see you in a few days, okay?"

"Sounds perfect, dear. And you should bring Garrett. We haven't seen him in a long time."

I could tell it was more of a demand than a request. "Okay, I'll ask him, but I can't guarantee anything. He's just started dating this girl, so I don't know that he'll want to spend an evening with me and my parents."

"Oh, really? I'm surprised he's... found time to start dating anyone. Either way, I'm sure he'll want to come."

"If you say so. I really gotta go, though. Love you, and send Dad my love."

"We love you too, Ella. See you in a few days!"

I heard Armeta hang up before taking the phone away from my ear. I always found it funny how they sometimes 'requested' that I bring Garrett around. As great of a guy as he was, the only thing I could figure for why they wanted to see him was so that they could see how we interacted with each other to make sure things hadn't gotten too friendly between us. I found myself hoping he would say no.

Four loads of laundry later, the repetitiveness hit me, and I was suddenly exhausted. It was close to midnight, and I had an early class the next morning. I was starting to gather my things when I heard the bell above the entrance signal someone's arrival. I glanced up without really looking and returned to folding my final dryer load.

"Don't tell me you're done already?" The voice was incredibly close behind me, and it would have startled me had it not been so familiar.

"What happened to your date? Gidget, was it?"

Garrett laughed. "Bridget. I already walked her home."

My insides danced. "So, it didn't go too well?"

He started loading a machine. "No, it went fine. I told you, I wanted to start dating someone. I'm not gonna sleep with her the first night. You know I'm not that kind of guy."

The dancing feet inside me started kicking my heart and then I mentally kicked myself for letting it affect me this way. "Maybe true, but we both know you need to get some. You're about to screw anything that walks," I teased.

"Well, not anything. Just a few certain women." He winked at me, and I turned away quickly.

"I wish you would have gotten here sooner. I'm so tired, and I have a class practically right after the sun comes up tomorrow. I can't stay any longer." I yawned.

He looked at my laundry bag. "But you aren't even done yet. You still have at least one load there."

"I know, but I have to get to bed." I frowned. I knew if I didn't do it tonight, I wouldn't get to it for a long time. He knew that too.

"Just leave it here. I'll take care of it and bring it over tomorrow."

"I don't know, Garrett," I started.

"Relax, Ella. It's just laundry."

"I know, but I can't guarantee what's in there."

Garrett laughed. "Is a monster going to jump out and bite me?"

I blushed a little as I replied, "No, but a bra clasp might."

Garrett quickly shut up. "Oh. Well. Don't even worry about it. It's not like I've never handled a bra before."

I had an internal battle—*it was a bad idea* versus *it needed to get done and I was too tired.* Ultimately, the latter won. "Fine. I'll be home around five. Can you bring it by then?"

"Absolutely. I'll see you then."

"Great. Oh, and before I forget, I'm going to my parents' later this week to bake cookies for an event. They wanted me to ask you to join me. Seems they miss you for some odd reason."

"I wouldn't miss it for the world, Ella. You know that. And you know I love your cookies. I claim all taste testing responsibility."

I snickered. "Of course you do, but you have to leave some cookies for the event. And are you sure Gidget—"

"Bridget," he interrupted.

"Are you sure she won't mind you hanging out with another girl and going to her parents'?"

"We've only been out once. She has no right for it to bother her. And besides, you and I are just friends. Remember?"

I thought I heard a bit of animosity at his last remark, but I convinced myself that I had imagined it. "Right.

Okay. Thanks for helping with my laundry." I smiled at him. "Goodnight."

He offered a goodnight in return as I headed out the door.

I overslept the next morning and had to rush to make it to my first class on time. I was happy to see that most of my classmates were the same as last semester. I heard that tended to happen when you got this many years into a major, but I wasn't sure if it would be true for biology students. I sat with the same group as I did last semester. Our professor was new to the university and rather uptight, so I didn't have much time to catch up with them.

I had one other class before Mythology, and I was again happy to see a familiar crowd. The professor was the student favorite in the department, so I had been very much looking forward to this class.

I went into my Mythology class not expecting to find anyone new, so I was surprised to see Austin sitting in the front row. I made my way to my usual place in the middle of the room and almost as soon as I sat down, Austin turned around and saw me. It was almost as if he could sense me. I smiled and waved, which he shyly returned before turning back to the front of the room.

Brandon came into the room shortly thereafter. He was sharply dressed in a lilac button-down oxford shirt with the top button undone so that his white undershirt was visible. The shirt was tucked into pressed khaki pants with a dark brown belt. His short brown hair was always perfectly styled, and his Rolex lookalike could always be found on his right wrist. He took his place at the podium and glanced around the room, nodding to the students who stuck with him instead of switching to the other Mythology professor. When his eyes met mine, he smiled and appeared to laugh a little.

Once he finished a sweep of the room, he decided to pick on me. "I see you've assumed your usual location, Miss Birch."

"I wouldn't have it any other way, Mr. Robbins."

"Still refusing to sit up front then?" he asked. "I would think an engaged student such as yourself would sit front row."

"Well, with an enthusiastic teacher like you, it could be downright dangerous to sit too close."

"I don't know what you are talking about, Ella." He purposefully exaggerated his arm movements as he spoke. I often wondered if he was Italian with how much he spoke with his hands.

"Of course you don't, Brandon. You tend to be oblivious like that." I saw a few people look at me funny when I addressed him by his first name. They must have been the students who took the other professor during the last semester.

"You may have a point," he smiled. He looked at the students in the front row. "You should probably move farther back."

Slowly, as though no one wanted to be the first to move in case he was kidding, the students in front gathered their things and moved back a few rows. Some moved all the way to the back of the room. Austin came and sat in the row behind me.

Once everyone was settled again, Brandon began explaining his syllabus and then jumped into a lecture. He decided to start the semester with *The Odyssey*.

"So, the sailors tied Odysseus to the mast and covered their ears so they wouldn't be able to hear their song. Who has thoughts on this?"

One of the new students raised her hand. He asked her name and told her she needn't raise her hand but can just call out her answer or thought. He explained that he liked to keep his class more like a conversation than a Q&A.

"I think he is a masochist."

"You may have something there. Having to hear the Siren's song while knowing he couldn't go to these beautiful women is a bit masochistic," Brandon responded.

I smiled. Everyone assumed Sirens were beautiful women, but I knew that wasn't true. "Who says they have to be beautiful?"

Brandon laughed. "Homer, for one."

"And you're going to take the word of an ancient poet?"

"Oh, this should be good. And what makes you think they weren't beautiful women?"

"What guy do you know that would need to hear a beautiful song to convince them to run to a beautiful woman?"

"Touché. What do you propose they were like then?"

I worded my reply carefully. "I would imagine they were absolute old hags who required men to maintain their immortality."

One of the men in the class quickly jumped in. "What's the point of living forever if you're absolutely hideous?"

A beautiful girl a few rows away from him responded, "Wouldn't you want to live forever if you could?"

"Of course! That would be awesome!" He obviously didn't get where she was going with it.

"But what's the point?" she finished.

There was a sweeping, "Oooohh!" from the class, and the guy shrunk in his seat.

"Okay, guys. Calm down," Brandon started. "Thanks for the perspective, Ella. Interesting and intriguing as always."

I smiled in return.

Austin leaned forward and whispered in my ear, "Interesting theory."

"Thanks," I replied.

"It's almost as if you know this stuff firsthand or something."

I shifted uncomfortably in my chair. "Nope. Just like to play Devil's advocate and put Mr. Robbins on the spot." I decided not to participate for the remainder of the lecture.

Brandon used the last ten minutes of class to have us sign up for a meeting with him to discuss our term paper topics. He did this every semester so he wouldn't have to read about the same thing in every paper or the usual suspects, like Aphrodite and Hades.

I was one of the last to make it to the signup sheet, and none of the time slots left worked with my schedule, as usual. I waited for the rest of the class to leave. When I opened my mouth to speak, Brandon beat me to it. "Let me guess. None of those times work for you."

"Ah, you know me too well."

He sighed, but not out of irritation. "And as usual, do you already have a topic picked out?"

"Actually, no. I want to think about it for a while."

Brandon suddenly smiled. "Oh, great. Well, when do you want to talk about it? I'm sure I can work around your schedule. Maybe we could meet for coffee and discuss it?"

I wasn't sure what to think. It sounded like he was asking me out, but I thought there was no way that could have been what just happened. "Actually, it would be easier for me if you could come by my work right around closing time. Tomorrow would be perfect if you can make it."

"When's closing time?"

"Around five. It's right on campus, just a little south of here. Make a left at the first road, and it'll be there on your left."

"My last class lets out at six. I wouldn't be able to make it."

"Oh, that's no problem. I can stay late and wait. I have plenty to do there anyway."

Brandon smiled. "You sure your boss won't mind?"

I was confused at first at the concept of a boss. "Oh, Brandon. You don't know me as well as I thought you did."

He raised an eyebrow and gave me a perplexed look.

"I *am* the boss. I own the business. Well, co-own. Me and my friend Garrett started it up in high school out of my house. When we came to campus and I saw that building was available, I jumped on it."

"Oh. Wow. That's impressive, Ella."

I blushed as I started toward the door. "I'll see you at six-ish tomorrow."

"I wouldn't miss it."

With my classes done for the day, I walked across the street to my apartment building and found Garrett outside smoking. He was dressed in his ridiculous running clothes that looked like they belonged in the eighties.

"Finishing or starting?" I asked him, as I approached.

"Starting, of course. I'd never smoke after a run. I'd hardly be able to breathe!"

I laughed at the irony of his statement. "Do you mind waiting a little bit so I can join you?"

"I don't know, Ella. You might slow me down."

"Doubtful," I replied, watching the tip of his cigarette glow orange as he took another deep inhale.

Thinking it'd be funny to join his eighties theme, I ran up to my apartment and threw on a pair of black leggings and an oversized neon purple shirt. The straps of the black sports bra I changed into were visible on my shoulders. I smiled to myself as I climbed back down the stairs.

CHAPTER 7

When I came back outside he was finishing his stretches. He had his right hand touching his left shoulder with his elbow bent behind his head. My eyes lingered on his muscles. They seemed bigger than I'd previously noticed, and it looked like the sleeves of his t-shirt could hardly contain them. I composed myself, then stood next to him and lifted my heel to the back of my thigh, holding my ankle to keep it in place. I switched to the other leg as he switched arms.

"You ready?" he asked.

"Almost."

I spread my feet slightly and bent in half so that my fingertips touched the cement in between them.

"Damn, Ella, warn a guy."

I turned my head and looked up at him just as he tore his eyes from my ass sticking up in the air. "What?"

"What, what?"

"You just said 'damn,'" I told him, as I straightened out.

"Oh. I said that out loud?"

"You sure did. So, damn what?"

"Damn, you take too long. Let's go." He started running down the street before I could respond.

I caught up quickly and kept pace with him. We ran in silence, but instead of being awkward, it was comforting. It was a beautiful fall day and the leaves had already changed colors and were beginning to fall. A few trees had already lost all of their leaves while others were still mostly green. When we made it to the other end of campus, we continued on into the neighborhood. I tried to focus on my run so I wouldn't feel the need to heal anything, but my curiosity got the best of me. I made sure to let Garrett pull ahead of me when we were passing a flower bed that was in dire need. As I ran past it, I allowed my hand to brush overtop of the drooping blooms, and they were immediately invigorated and vibrant with life.

After a few miles, we headed back to our building. When we reached our destination, Garrett sounded like he was hyperventilating. I was also out of breath, but not nearly as badly. "I see what you mean about not being able to smoke afterward," I teased.

"Very... funny... Ella."

"Race you up the stairs?"

"Hell... no. Elevator."

While waiting for the elevator doors to open at my floor, I told him to bring my clothes by once he was able to breathe again. When I got into my apartment, I began cooking dinner, making sure to make enough for Garrett. He was always ravenous after a run. He walked in right as I was turning off the stove.

"You know, you really should lock that. I could have been a burglar or a rapist."

"I knew you'd be here."

"So, what if someone else came first?"

"Then, when you got here, you'd kick their ass and protect me."

He shrugged. "Fair enough. What's for dinner?" he asked, as he threw my laundry bag on my bed.

I saw that he had folded my clothes and was grateful that I wouldn't have to. I absolutely hated folding laundry.

"Stuffed peppers. There wasn't anything too embarrassing in there, was there?" I asked, pointing at my bag.

He laughed, and his cheeks turned slightly pink. "Only if you're embarrassed by bras and panties. There wasn't any lingerie or anything."

I wanted to fade away into the wall. He probably wouldn't even have noticed what everything was had he not folded the clothes. Now, I had an image burned in my mind of him picking up a pair of my panties and putting them in my bag, followed by the matching bra. Maybe he wouldn't notice if I made my plants conceal me.

"Why would there be lingerie? I'm not dating anyone."

"Don't ruin every guy's fantasy that girls wear lingerie all the time when they are home alone. Or when they have their girlfriends over," he teased.

"Oh. Yes. Of course. All lingerie, all the time. How could I forget?"

"That's more like it! Now, I vote you go put on that black striped bra with the pink lace and matching panties and then we can eat."

I felt my face turn eight shades of red. "I don't think your girlfriend would appreciate you talking to another woman like that."

"Jesus, Ella. She's not my girlfriend, and she never will be, for that matter, if she isn't confident enough to be okay with me joking around with a good friend."

"So, no second date then? Did you decide you didn't like her after all?" I pried.

"No. I just haven't had the chance to call her yet. I planned on getting to that tonight. Unless you know of some reason I shouldn't?"

"Just eat your food," I ordered and dug into my own. He eventually asked me about my day and my classes. I told him about Austin and about how Brandon was going to be coming by the office the next day.

"That's weird, Ella."

"I know! I don't understand how he just happened to look exactly where I was sitting. Owen met him and thought he was weird too. I wrote him off, but maybe he was onto something."

"While that is also weird, I wasn't talking about Austin. I was talking about your professor."

"Brandon? What's weird about him?"

"That you call him Brandon, for starters. I've never been on a first name basis with a teacher. And he asked you on a *date*."

I shook my head while finishing chewing my bite. "He did not ask me on a date. It just came across wrong. He's accommodating my schedule, and he knows I like coffee. And he has every student call him Brandon, not just me."

"Well, you should at least have him stop by during business hours, not afterhours."

"He has classes all day, and I have to stay late anyway. Now, finish your food before it gets cold and gross."

He scooped some rice onto his fork. "Fine. I'll stay and help you finish up. I wouldn't want to get to your parents' house too late tomorrow."

I sighed, and we finished dinner in silence. Afterward, I walked him to the door and hugged him. He squeezed me harder than usual, and I realized this was the first time we had hugged since we almost crossed the line. I had forgotten that I'd been avoiding hugs with him while he got over it. I supposed it was safe now that he had started dating someone, but then... he did hold me tighter and longer than usual.

The next day was incredibly busy at work. We had a Relay for Life event coming up that we were donating our services to, and that meant a lot of marketing materials had to be made and flyers had to be hung. On top of that, the university hired us for homecoming week. It was a big step for us as we had been trying to get the school to have our bins in every building. Despite our efforts, they had yet to sign a contract with us. We had managed to secure some of their smaller events, but nothing as major as homecoming.

My phone was constantly ringing, and it seemed like I was receiving emails faster than I could answer them. I was surprised when I looked up from my desk to see that Garrett was the only one left. I stood from my chair and made an attempt to stretch the stiffness out of my legs. After that didn't do much, I walked over to Garrett, who was surfing the internet.

"If you have nothing to do, you should go. There's no point in hanging around," I told him.

"I told you. I'm waiting for your teacher with you."

"Garrett, I'm an adult. I can take care of myself. You don't have to babysit me."

"So, you admit he wants you."

"What? No! I just know that's what you think is going to happen." The door opened as I was speaking, and Brandon walked in.

"What's going to happen?" he asked.

I smiled at him. "Hi, Brandon. I was just telling Garrett that he needs to go so he doesn't get behind on his homework like he does every semester."

"But—" Garrett started.

"No buts. Get out of here," I told him. When he didn't make to leave, I walked over to the door and held it open for him.

Finally, he started for the door. "Ella," he started when he reached me.

I lowered my voice. "I'll be fine. I'll stop by to get you before I go to my parents." Once he finally left, I turned my attention back to Brandon.

"You sure he's just your friend? He seems rather protective," Brandon said.

"Yeah, we're just friends. We've known each other since forever. How were today's classes?" I asked, eager to change the subject.

"Nowhere near as entertaining or pleasant as yesterday. Did you figure out what you want to write about?"

"Today has been so busy I haven't had any time to think."

"Well, I've met with a few people already, and Poseidon, Medusa, and Eros are already taken," he told me.

"I don't think I want to do something so well known."

"I wouldn't expect you to, Ella." He took a step closer to me.

"What do you suggest?"

"Well, you seemed pretty fond of the Sirens. Or there's always Nike. Oh! I'd love to hear your take on sex-crazed Nymphs."

Had I been drinking anything, I would have choked on it. Instead, I coughed incessantly.

Brandon raised an eyebrow. "I never pinned you as the type to laugh at talk of sex."

"I'm not. I take sex very seriously."

"Well, that doesn't sound fun," he teased.

"I, well, I mean. You know what I mean." I hated being flustered.

"No, I don't, actually. What *do* you mean?"

"I can be..." I looked down before finishing. "I can be fun."

Before I had a chance to raise my head, I heard Brandon say, "I'm sure you can." Then, his finger was beneath my chin, raising my face to his. Suddenly, his lips were crushing mine. There was a fire behind his kiss that surprised me. I didn't resist his advance, even though I knew I should. When I felt his lips part, I allowed mine to part in response. He tasted like peppermint and coffee.

Taking my reaction as permission, his hand made its way to the back of my head where he grabbed ahold of my hair. My body pressed into his, and my arms wrapped around his neck. His lips slowed down, and he gently and sweetly kissed me four times before pulling away. He rested his forehead against mine and whispered my name.

I had to work to slow down my breathing and uncloud my mind. I willed myself to take a step back. In doing so, his hand let go of my hair and dropped to his side.

"Is something wrong?" he asked.

"We should not have done that."

"It was amazing, Ella. Tell me you don't agree."

"You're my teacher."

"And we're both adults."

"Brandon. Please. It's just too complicated."

"It's not complicated at all."

"Please," I breathed.

He stared into my eyes for a moment, as though he was searching for something. "Okay. I'm sorry if I overstepped. We just have this great chemistry, and you are so damn beautiful."

"I'm sorry, Brandon. Really, I am."

"Don't even worry about it. Just email me your topic of choice. I'm sure I'll be fine with whatever you pick," he said, as he looked down at his shoes, avoiding further eye contact.

I could tell he was embarrassed.

I nodded my head, and he left. I took a few minutes to think about what had just happened. I thought about the feel of his lips moving with mine and his hand in my hair. I wondered if my response to him was because I was attracted to him or because it had been so long since I'd had that kind of physical contact.

When I finally headed outside into the cool evening air, I made sure to lock the door behind me before texting Owen to ask him to convince Elijah that it would be a good idea to ask me out.

I walked up to my apartment building and found Garrett waiting for me outside.

"So? How'd it go?" he asked.

"Fine," I lied.

"What did you decide?" he asked.

"I... what? What do you mean?"

"Your term paper. That he came by to discuss. Let me guess. You never got to that."

I sighed and put my key in the lobby door. "No, we did. I still haven't completely decided. But I'm probably going with the Sirens."

"Oh. Good. Are you ready to go, or do you need to run upstairs first?"

I elected to run up to my apartment and change into more comfortable clothes. A few minutes later, we were walking to the bus stop in near silence. Whenever Garrett asked me anything, I gave either an "uh-huh" or a "nuh-uh." When we were on the bus and I still hadn't said much, Garrett became concerned.

"You sure you're okay?" he asked.

"I'm fine, Garrett. Don't worry about it."

"I just haven't seen you this quiet in a long time. Probably not since you and Edgar broke up."

I thought about what he said. He was right. When Edgar and I broke up, I was quiet for over a week. That was different, though. That was depression. Edgar broke my heart. He was dating another girl within days of our breakup.

I wasn't depressed or heartbroken now. At least, I didn't think I was. I was just confused and lonely. I hadn't realized just how lonely I was until Brandon's kiss stirred things inside me.

"I've just got a lot on my mind. And a ton of cookies to bake tonight." I forced my eyes away from the window where I was watching the buildings blur by and put a smile on my face.

"What exactly are you baking these for?"

"An event tomorrow night," I told him.

"You already told me it was an event. What kind of event, though?" he pried.

I made an attempt to sidestep the question. "What does it matter? It's nothing exciting."

"Because sometimes you can be so mysterious about your life. I'm your best friend and business partner, and it seems like I don't know half of the things you spend your time on."

"I guess I didn't know you were that interested in the ins and outs of my life," I lied. "They are for a... family reunion. Armeta said the usual family baker wasn't going to be able to make it, so she asked me to fill in."

"With as good as your cookies are, I would think you'd be the normal family baker."

The bus finally reached our stop. "You are too sweet," I teased.

We stepped off the bus, and Aaron was waiting for us, leaned up against his usual tree. When he saw us, he took a step forward and held out his hand to shake Garrett's. "Hello, Garrett. It's good to finally see you again."

"You too, Aaron. Seems like it's been forever."

As we walked to the house, Aaron and Garrett chatted about everything from sports to school to plans for the future.

When we walked inside, Armeta greeted me with a hug before offering one to Garrett.

"Hey, Armeta. You look radiant as always," he said.

"Thank you, Garrett. And I dare say, you look more handsome every time we see you," Armeta replied.

"It's just an illusion," I teased.

Garrett pinched my side in response, causing me to squeal and jump away from him. I quickly looked at my parents and caught them exchanging a meaningful look. Garrett's behavior was not something that happened between friends who barely saw each other. He was unraveling my falsifications and destroying my credibility.

Garrett continued his small talk as though nothing significant had transpired. "So, I hear your normal baker can't make it to the reunion."

"Reunion?" Aaron asked, looking at me.

"Yeah, I was just telling him why I had to bake so many cookies tonight. For the reunion tomorrow," I explained.

"Oh, right," Armeta agreed. "We usually just call it a Gathering."

Aaron smiled a knowing smile.

Clueless, Garrett nodded his head. "I like it. No one ever wants to go to a reunion. Calling it a family gathering takes some of the pressure off. And I know I have no say since I'm not in the family, but for what it's worth, Ella ought to be the normal baker. Her cookies are the best I've ever had."

I wished I could punch him without drawing attention.

"We hadn't realized you were so well acquainted with Ella's cookies," Armeta said.

I quickly jumped in before Garrett could say anything else damaging. "Yeah, I make them for our employees from time to time." I glanced at Garrett and saw him give me a weird look. "Anyway, it's already pretty late. We should get started."

We all made our way into the kitchen, and I immediately dove into the task at hand. I was vaguely aware of the conversation going on. When I started hearing my name too often, I decided it was time to steer them in another direction.

"Garrett, why don't you tell them about Bridget? I'm sure they'd love to hear all about her."

He spent the next half hour or so telling them about her and answering their seemingly endless questions. When that topic was exhausted, he took a low blow. "Should I tell them about Brandon for you as well?"

Aaron and Armeta looked at me, but it was Aaron who spoke, "Who's Brandon?"

I cursed Garrett internally. "He's my Mythology teacher. Funny guy, and a great teacher. I was just explaining that to Garrett the other day at work, and he teased me about having a crush on him."

I quickly glanced at Garrett and saw him give me another weird look.

"Well, do you have a crush on him?" Armeta asked. "It would be perfectly normal if you did."

Garrett didn't catch the double meaning. Before tonight I would have been able to instantly say no, but now I wasn't sure. Even if I did like him, I'd never tell my parents, or Garrett, for that matter. So I hesitated slightly before answering. "No. He's just a great teacher." In hopes of ending this horrid topic, I added, "And besides, Owen said he's pretty sure Elijah is going to ask me out the next time he sees me."

To my parents, that meant tomorrow, but as far as Garrett knew, it could be days or weeks.

"Who's Elijah?" Garrett asked. "Was he at the bar with us the other night?"

I about wanted to cut off Garrett's tongue. "Yeah, that was so weird that we ran into you and Tracy that night. Elijah was the one with dark hair, sitting across from Owen."

"Oh, right," he agreed. I doubted he knew who I was talking about. We spent most of that night zoned into each other and didn't pay much attention to anyone else there. I was grateful he played along instead of exposing my now tangled web of lies.

I took the first batch of cookies out of the oven, and Aaron poured everyone a glass of milk. We each ate a cookie after they had cooled down enough.

"Perfect, as usual," Garrett offered.

As I continued making more batches, we ended up finishing a bottle of wine, and Armeta cooked Garrett and I some dinner when she found out we hadn't eaten yet. Garrett seemed to have gotten the hint and didn't go into why we missed dinner. It was around midnight when we finally said our goodbyes. Armeta gave each of us a hug, and Aaron shook Garrett's hand again before hugging me goodbye.

As we were walking down the path to the sidewalk, Garrett said, "I love your parents. They're so warm and welcoming."

"Yeah, they're pretty great," I agreed.

"Too bad they don't feel the same way about me, though."

"Why do you say that?" I asked.

"It seems to me like you don't want them knowing how close we are. Based on how you twisted everything tonight, I'd guess they think we are pretty much just coworkers and not friends."

"Ah. You noticed that then? It's not that they don't like you, Garrett. I promise."

"Then, why do you lie to them?"

"I just don't want them getting the wrong idea about us. They are hopeless romantics. They'd be rooting for the romantic comedy ending where the girl next door ends up with the boy best friend," I explained, even though I didn't believe it to be true one bit.

"Right. And since that'll never happen..."

"Exactly."

"Is that why you made up that business about Elijah? To give them someone else to focus their attention on?"

"No, I didn't make that up. He probably is going to ask me out soon."

We reached the bus stop just as the bus was about to pull up. "Oh," he said. "And what are you going to tell him?"

"I don't know. It depends on what he says. 'Yes, I'll go to the movies with you.' 'No, I don't think 9:00pm is too late for coffee,'" I told him as we got on the bus.

"You're such a smart ass. So, you like this kid then?"

"He's not a kid, Garrett. He's actually a few years older than us. And I hadn't thought about it much before, but I'm willing to give it a try."

"You talk about him like he's some product you can try out and return if you don't like it."

"You know what I mean. I haven't dated anyone in a while, and I think I'm ready to start."

"Why now?" he asked.

"I don't know. I guess I'm just lonely."

"You've got to be kidding me." He sounded defeated.

"I mean, I miss that physical contact. And before you get all pervy on me, I don't just mean sex. And I miss that connection that you get when you're dating someone."

"Ella..." he started. "Never mind."

"You wouldn't get it. You're a guy."

"How does my being a guy mean I wouldn't get it?" The bus came to a stop, and we got off and headed to our building.

"Because. Girls are the more romantic of the sexes. We look for connections and the little things that show us a guy cares. Guys look for sex and a sense of humor. And beauty."

"Not all of us. Some of us want that connection too. We want the long conversations about everything, the small gestures that no one else would notice. Hell, we even sometimes want the long walks on the beach."

I tried not to laugh as he held the door open for me, and we headed to the stairwell. "You're right. Some guys do want all that, and hopefully, Elijah is one of those guys."

"Why can't I be that guy?" he asked quietly.

"Garrett. Stop. We're not going over this again."

He quickly deflected. "Easy, Birch. I meant, I hope I can be that guy for Gidget."

"Bridget," I corrected him with a smile.

"Damn it."

We had reached my floor and were now standing just inside the drab hallway. "Goodnight, Garrett. I'll see you later."

"Goodnight, Ella," he said while pulling me into a hug. He kissed my cheek, his whiskers scratching my skin. As he pulled away, he added, "Sweet dreams."

My cheek felt like it was on fire, a desire churning inside of me. "You too."

I walked away from him, eager to go to bed. It had been such a long, weird day, and with any luck, I'd be getting asked on a date the next night.

When I got into my apartment, I watered my plants and fell into bed, too tired to change into pajamas.

CHAPTER 8

The next day I rode the bus to the Gathering with Emma and Arthur. They held hands the whole time but seemed annoyed with each other. When we made it to the clearing, I found my way to my parents. They were deep in a serious conversation with some of their friends that I didn't know very well. I figured it best not to interrupt, so I scanned the crowd for Owen. He was talking to Elijah. When I looked over at him, Owen glanced my way and smiled. I took that as a sign that convincing Elijah was going well.

I hated the headspace I was in today and found it difficult to concentrate on the beautiful nature that surrounded me. I barely noticed the chirping birds or the bickering squirrels that were probably fighting over one of the few remaining acorns that they were both trying to store for the winter.

Owen motioned at me to join them. On my way over,
I heard hushed conversations. Something was going on,
and it didn't look good.

"Hey, Ella. Do you want to go for a walk with us
before the ceremony starts?" Owen asked.

"That sounds perfect. I need to see my tree, and I'd
rather not do it with a big crowd."

We set off down the path and made our way to the
tree I had been healing. I approached it and put both of
my hands against her bark. She had done some healing
on her own, and I could feel a residual effect from my last
offering still coursing through her. I offered her more
energy, and she willingly took it into her trunk as I
directed it to repair some internal damage.

"That's amazing," Elijah said, as I stepped back. "You
come out here every time and help her?"

"Yeah. Every chance I get."

He smiled at me. "Would you mind?" he asked, as he
took a step toward her.

"Of course not, the more help she gets, the better.
She's almost completely healed. Maybe the infusion of
your energy on top of mine will do the trick."

With that, he stepped forward and placed a hand upon her bark. I watched in amazement as he provided all he could. I'd only seen a handful of other Nymphs perform healings, as it was considered an intimate moment, and therefore was usually done in private. Adding to my amazement, he was able to give more energy and make it more pinpointed than I could because he was a few years older than me.

"It wasn't quite enough," he said. "But I imagine she'll need just a few more offerings now."

"Thank you so much, Elijah. That's very kind of you."

"We should probably get back before they start." Owen's voice startled me. I had almost forgotten he was there.

We made it back to the clearing just as the cleansing sticks were being lit. The opening prayer was said, and I danced alongside Owen and Elijah. Once the fire was smoking after everyone had deposited their cleansing sticks, Ursula provided the first blessing.

I dug my toes into the ground in anticipation of the electric sensation. It coursed through my body and awakened every nerve. My fingers tingled much in the same way they did after Garrett held my hand. I thought I could even feel my hair buzzing with the energy. I closed my eyes and watched an explosion of color dance across my eyelids. I could feel the energy begin its return to the earth, and in an effort to slow it down, I stood on the balls of my feet. I opened my eyes just as Eugene started speaking.

"Today is a somber day. We Gather, as we always have, in our sacred place. However, this evening we have difficult news to share." He looked to Ursula.

"We had hoped the events we are about to speak of were coincidental. At this time, it appears there is a pattern that can no longer be ignored," she said.

I looked around the circle and across the fire. Some of the adults were giving knowing nods, including Aaron and Armeta. Others, and most of the younger members, looked around as I did, with worry and confusion etched into their faces.

Olivia spoke next. "Over the past several months, four Nymphs have gone missing. The most recent disappearance was only a few days before our last Gathering. We did not speak of it then because we had not had the chance to discuss the circumstances regarding the disappearance with the Elders of the affected clan. Now that we have, we believe it is prudent that we share this information." She looked to Ian.

"All four of the Nymphs that have gone missing have been female," Ian added. "We do not believe this is the work of a satyr but have not ruled out the possibility."

One of the adults spoke up. "If it's women who have gone missing, why have you decided it likely wasn't a satyr?"

Ian avoided his question. "You can relax, Ephraim. We believe Ivory will be safe." He was speaking of Ephraim's charge. "As I said, the missing Nymphs are all female, however, that is not the only thing they have in common."

As though I felt their eyes on me, I looked over at my parents and found them staring at me. Armeta had tears in her eyes, and Aaron had welled up as well.

Ursula continued, "These women were also born of the same forest. We believe they are looking for a particular Nymph and do not know how to identify her from afar. It seems they are randomly capturing Nymphs of this forest, and they somehow manage to figure out if she is who they are looking for after they have her."

"We believe that the missing have been murdered when it was discovered they were not the one they were looking for," Eugene said to many gasps. "We also hope we can discover who or what is behind these disappearances before another Nymph goes missing."

"What forest are they fixated on?" Emma asked.

I looked back at my parents and got a lump in my throat. I was pretty sure I already knew the answer.

Eugene looked at Emma with kind eyes. He knew we were good friends and that this would have an impact on her as well. "The Smoky Mountain forests, my dear child."

"Then, our clan is safe, right? No one here was born there," Emma said confidently.

Owen grabbed Emma's hand, much to Arthur's dismay. "Emma, honey, Ella was born from that forest."

My heart sank. I heard Armeta sob quietly into Aaron's shoulder. I didn't have the strength to look at her. It would make me cry right along with her.

"There's no way," Emma said. "Tell them, Ella." She turned to me. "Tell them that isn't where you were born."

I looked her in the eyes. They were frantic. Probably trying to search her memory for where I was born. "I was," I squeaked.

"But... You... You never told me. Why have you never told me that?"

"You never asked," I replied simply.

Emma quickly turned on Owen and jerked her hand from his. "And how do you know where she's from?"

"Now is not the time, Emma," Owen said.

Ursula quickly jumped in. "No, and we all need to come together now. Just because Ella may be the only target among us does not mean the rest of us are safe. We must all be diligent. Do not travel alone, and be sure to lock your doors and keep your energy up." She looked directly at me, which caused me to shiver. "There's no telling what lengths this person will go to in order to get what he wants. Until we know his motives, we will not be able to anticipate his actions."

"May the Goddess Artemis be with us all," Eugene prayed.

Just what I needed. Some supernatural stalker that wanted to do who knew what to me. Because my life wasn't already complicated enough.

"I know we normally take some time to hear from everyone, but under the circumstances, we think it's best to end the ceremony early tonight. Everyone can talk amongst themselves about how they plan on keeping their neighborhood safe and how others can help that effort," Eugene said.

Olivia offered the closing blessing.

I stooped down and grabbed handfuls of dirt. As I spread it across my arms, repeating the blessing, I felt my skin crawl with electricity and fear. It was one thing to be under attack, but to not know why, or who the enemy was, or from which direction the attack was coming was unsettling.

As soon as everyone started queuing up for the food, Owen pulled me into an embrace. "You better watch out, Ella. I can't lose my sister."

"Stop it, Owen. I'll be fine." I saw Aaron and Armeta approaching. "Help me be strong. Armeta is going to make me cry if I'm not careful." I took a deep breath as he nodded.

As soon as Armeta was within arm's reach, she pulled me into a hug, and Aaron wrapped his arms around the both of us.

"How long have you known about this?" I asked.

"We heard about the disappearances as they happened," Aaron said. "But we just heard about the forest connection when we got here tonight. The Elders didn't want us to be blindsided when they announced it."

"How considerate of them. Guess it doesn't matter if they blindsided me. After all, I should get used to it since I apparently have to be ready for anything."

"Stop it," Armeta said. "They probably would have told you if you had gotten here sooner."

I shrugged.

"Ella, I don't want you going anywhere alone. Make Garrett walk you to class if you have to. And to work. It would really be best if you didn't live alone, either. Maybe Emma could stay with you for a while?"

I shook my head. "I don't think that's a good idea. She's already mad at me about not telling her what forest I'm from. Now with Owen announcing his knowledge of it, she's gonna be furious."

"Then, what about Garrett? Just tell him we're worried about you living all alone. I'm sure he'd be willing to help."

"Maybe a little too willing," Owen joked, only loud enough for me to hear.

I elbowed him in the side when my parents weren't looking.

"Armeta," Aaron started. Clearly, he didn't like the idea of me living with Garrett. And he probably picked up on the closeness of our relationship that I had hidden from them. Maybe even some of the sexual tension between us.

"I'll do it," Owen announced.

"Do what?" I asked, and at the same time Armeta said, "Oh, wonderful!"

"Stay with you, silly. I'm worried about you too. And you'd be much safer with a man living with you." He looked at Aaron. "And I'm sure Aaron would be more comfortable knowing a brother-figure was staying with you than some other man."

Aaron nodded his approval.

"I don't need a babysitter, guys. I'm a big girl. I can take care of myself."

Armeta's eyes started tearing up again. "Please, Ella. It'll make me feel so much better. Or you could move back home with us for a while," she offered.

I sighed. "Fine. Owen can move in. Hope you like the couch."

He smiled at me, and Armeta took him into a tight hug. "Thank you so much, Owen. You have no idea how much it means to us."

I rolled my eyes. My fear had now been replaced with annoyance. "Let's go for a walk, Owen."

"Sure. Let me just grab Elijah."

I met them by the path into the forest. Our friends saw us headed that way and followed. A lot of them gave me sad looks and patted my back, telling me it would be okay. I felt like they were treating me as though I had a terminal illness. Emma gave me a dirty look as she passed by, dragging Arthur with her. He didn't look happy, either. I waited for everyone to pass by so the three of us could be alone.

"Please tell me you have your own stash," I said to Owen.

"Of course I do." He smiled and pulled a joint out of his pocket.

I grabbed it from him greedily, and Elijah held out a lighter to its end. "Thanks," I murmured, the joint bouncing in my mouth.

He lit the end, and I inhaled as though I hadn't taken a breath in hours. The smoke seared my throat on the way down, and although my lungs already felt like they were at capacity, I took another hit before holding it out for someone else to grab. It was already a quarter of the way gone, so when Elijah grabbed it from me, his fingers touched mine. He caught my eye and smiled before taking a hit.

My head was swirling, and my lungs burned. It felt as though every air pocket in them was being singed, and yet it felt good. My eyes started watering, and I had a feeling my face was turning purple. Finally, I exhaled slowly, and the smoke poured out from between my lips. I took a deep breath of fresh air and could taste the decomposing leaves that blanketed the ground. I could smell the must in the air and wanted to bathe in it.

Owen handed the joint back to me, his cheeks puffed out as he held his breath. I took another large hit and offered the remaining bit to Elijah.

"You can kill it. I think you probably need it more than us," he said.

Owen nodded his agreement, so I took one last hit before putting it out under my foot. I watched the wind blow through the trees, rustling every leaf that remained attached. As another large breeze came through, I let the smoke leave my lungs, and I watched as it danced away from us. This time, the air tasted like honey and tree sap. It was a wonderful mix. I wished I could bottle it and take it with me everywhere I went.

"Do you taste that?" I asked.

Owen laughed, shaking his head.

I approached an oak tree and sat at her base. When I leaned against her, it felt like her arms wrapped around me. I collected some of the dead leaves and dirt around her roots and rubbed them on my arms. I could feel the electricity again, and it was so powerful, I thought it might brand me. Elijah sat next to me, and Owen wandered some distance away.

"You have to feel this," I told Elijah and rubbed the earth and leaves across his arms. "Do you feel that?"

His arm jerked back. "Whoa! That's amazing. I've never felt anything like that before. What did you do to it?"

I shrugged. "It always feels like that to me. But this is more powerful. This is like searing my arms. But in a good way."

"Wow. That must be so awesome to be able to feel that every time. I'd be dirty twenty-four, seven."

I laughed, and he laughed with me. "It's so beautiful here. All the birds singing, and the leaves blowing. And the air tastes like honey and tree sap." I looked up. "And look at that sky! It's freaking orange! More orange than anything I've ever seen."

"Yeah," he agreed. "The sun must be setting. We should probably get back before people start to worry about you."

I heard myself sigh, but my lungs didn't feel it. This made me laugh again. "You're probably right. Where's Owen?"

"He went ahead. He'd be in the clearing by now."

"Why did he do that?" I asked.

"So, we could be alone." He tucked a strand of hair behind my ear.

"Why do we need to be alone?" I knew the plan was for Elijah to ask me out, but I figured all this business about the disappearing women would have scared him off. Even if it didn't, I still didn't understand why we had to be alone.

Another breeze blew through, and I turned my face
to it. It smelled like water saturated with heavy minerals,
and it made me thirsty.

"I guess he wanted to give us privacy in case I wanted
to kiss you," Elijah said.

"Oh. Do you want to kiss me?"

"I've always wanted to kiss you, Ella. The real
question is if you want me to kiss you."

No sooner than I nodded my head, his lips were
pressed against mine. He tasted like ginger and pot.
Letting my body take control, I straddled him and kissed
him deeper. When my tongue ventured into his mouth,
he tasted like full blown pumpkin pie. It was intoxicating
and gave me the munchies something fierce.

After some unknown space of time, I pried myself
away from him and stood up. He readjusted himself
before standing with me. I had to suppress a giggle.

We started walking back to the clearing, hand in hand.
He would occasionally lift my hand to his mouth and kiss
my fingers. I wondered what I tasted like to him.
Probably dirt since I had just been digging in it. We were
almost to the clearing, and I could hear Emma's voice.

She was talking quietly, but the voice responding to her was loud and angry.

"That's bullshit, Emma. You're still in love with him. It's obvious. I don't know what kind of person you are. Who does that to someone? Who breaks up with a man they are in love with to mess around with another?" He paused for effect, and she didn't say anything. "Oh, wait! I know! A filthy wh—"

"Hey!" I interrupted much louder than I probably should have. "Don't talk to her like that!"

"Please, Ella. Stay out of this," Emma pleaded.

"Yeah, Ella. Butt the fuck out! This isn't your business. You know what, why don't you just give yourself up to the kidnapper and spare us all the threat?"

Emma slapped Arthur across the face. I'd never seen anything like it. I'd seen her playfully smack Owen a few times, but those were like butterfly landings compared to this. His face instantly went red where she made contact, and an outline of her hand started taking shape.

"That's out of line, Arthur," she hissed. "Now, get out of here, and I better never see you again, so help me God."

Arthur looked betrayed but ran off. I couldn't believe I had ever felt sorry for him. Emma looked at me with an apology in her eyes, and I burst out laughing. It was a delayed reaction to watching Arthur run away like a bat out of hell. Emma smiled at me and started laughing as well.

We made it back to the clearing, and almost everyone was gone, as was all of the food.

The giant smile left my face, and I let go of Elijah's hand. Aaron and Armeta were hovering by the exit path, looking anxious. They were talking to Owen while looking around for me. When they saw me, I waved, and the tension left their faces. They smiled at me and hugged Owen, saying a few things to him. He nodded and reassured them until they finally left. As Owen made his way over to us, I turned to Emma and opened my mouth to speak.

She held her hand up. "Don't worry, Ella. All is forgiven. Of course you guys became friends. You were forced into hanging out so much, it was bound to happen."

"I'm glad you feel that way. And hopefully, you still will after you hear the most recent development."

Owen approached then, and I told her about our new living arrangement. Her face dropped, and her nostrils flared.

"Armeta asked him to. You know how she can be. She wanted a man staying with me to make her feel like I'll be safer."

She looked at Owen and exhaled a breath. "It's fine. Why should I care? I'm not with Owen anymore. And besides," she looked at my hand in Elijah's, which I hadn't even realized he'd grabbed again, "looks like you've got yourself a boyfriend now anyway. If anyone should be bothered, it's him."

Of course Emma was going to try to start some drama. Trying to plant the seed of jealousy in Elijah's head since she wasn't 'allowed' to be jealous herself.

I looked at Elijah, and he smiled at me, asking, "Since all the food's gone, what do you say we grab a bite to eat?"

"Absolutely. I'm starving. And I could use a drink." I turned to Emma and Owen. "You guys want to join us? We can go to that bar right on campus. They have great food."

"Sure," Owen said, and Emma nodded.

We rode the bus back in silence. I had my head leaned on Elijah's shoulder and started thinking about the Elders' warnings. I pictured a two headed monster stalking the shadows, waiting to eat me. I quickly shook that image from my head and concentrated on the feeling of Elijah's hand wrapped around mine. Before I knew it, the bus reached our stop and we parted ways to change before meeting at the bar. Elijah insisted on walking me to my door and picking me up from it afterward.

CHAPTER 9

When we got to the bar, we ordered food and dived in as soon as it arrived at the table. I must have drank three glasses of water before I had finished my plate. I hoped Elijah wouldn't hold this against me. After all, we missed dinner and I had the munchies.

I got back from the bathroom, and Elijah took me out on the dance floor. We were dancing and kissing and laughing. As I pulled away from a rather intense kiss, I opened my eyes and saw Garrett standing across the room, eyes wide as though he had seen a ghost. I excused myself from Elijah and approached him.

"That happened fast," Garrett said.

"What are you doing here?"

"Emma invited me. Or rather, she said you told her to invite me. But now I can't figure out why. Did you want to show off your new boyfriend?" His jaw clenched.

"No, Garrett. You know I wouldn't flaunt that around in front of you." I took a deep breath and wished I could turn my filter on. "Give me some credit. I'm not that mean. I know how you feel about me. I may act like I don't, but I do. And I'd never intentionally rub it in your face that I'm with someone else. I'm more discreet than that."

Garrett looked at me in what looked like shock. "And yet, here you are, making out with another guy in public."

"I didn't know you'd be here! I didn't think you even knew this place existed!"

"And doesn't it tell you something that you went through the trouble to go somewhere you knew I wouldn't be? If you didn't love me too, you wouldn't care if I saw you with another man."

"Garrett, please. I've had a rough night. Let's not do this. I just want to relax and have fun. I care about you, and I don't like hurting your feelings. That's all it is. Don't read more into it."

"Whatever you have to tell yourself, Ella. I'll see you at work Monday," he said and then left.

I went back to Elijah and dragged him back to the table. Emma was sitting there with a smile on her face, and Owen looked concerned.

"What is wrong with you, Emma? How can you purposely hurt someone like that?" I wanted to smack her like she smacked Arthur.

"What's going on?" Elijah asked. "Who was that?"

"That," Emma explained, "is the human who is in love with Ella."

"Why did you tell him I invited him here?"

"Because he wouldn't come if he knew I was the one inviting him."

"And why did you invite him? Do you hate him that much?"

"Ella, chill out. He's just a human. He needs to see that you're with someone and will never be with him. I just ripped the bandaid off. It was more humane than slowly picking at it like you were."

"I was handling it fine! He's got a girlfriend now. He's moved on! What you did was just cruel. He may be human, but he's still a person! And he's my best friend, or at least he was."

Emma looked hurt. "I'm your best friend, Ella. Me. Not him. He doesn't even know who you are. He only sees a small percentage of who you are because of that ridiculous business you started with him."

"No, Emma. We're done. You crossed the line." I got up to leave, and Elijah followed me. When we were outside, I leaned against the cool brick of the building and tried not to cry.

Elijah put his hands on my shoulders. "Hey. Don't let it get to you so bad. People have their hearts broken every day. You can't control who falls in love with you."

I looked up into his dark brown eyes. They were warm and kind. "It's not just that. I'm so stressed out as it is, and on top of that, Emma betrayed me."

"She has a small point," he said. "While his feelings aren't less important because he's human, you don't need to care about them so much. Best friend or not, it's not like you're in love with him too. He needed to get that message."

I sighed. "You may be right, but he's still my friend, and I still have to work with him. That's why I haven't ripped the bandaid off. I don't want to hurt him unnecessarily, and it would make every day at work awkward. I love my job. I don't want to dread going to work."

Owen came outside then. "Ella, I'll talk to Garrett. I'll let him know what happened. I'll let him know it's not your fault."

"Thanks, Owen."

"I'm going to go grab a few things from home, then I'll be over, okay?"

Elijah cleared his throat. "Actually, if Ella has no objection, I thought I could maybe keep watch tonight. After all, our first date sort of got ruined, and I'd like the chance to turn it around."

Owen looked at me for an answer, and I nodded. "Okay," he said. "Then, I'll come by in the morning, and we can go get signatures for that petition."

"Sounds great. I'll see you in the morning."

Owen waved and headed back into the bar. I hoped he was going to yell at Emma. She never pulled stuff like this when she was dating him, so maybe that meant he could keep her in line.

Elijah and I walked to my apartment building and up the stairs. When I opened my door, he looked around. "Cozy," he said.

"Yeah, it's not the biggest, but it's all I need."

We sat on the couch and turned on the TV. After flipping through a few channels, I stopped on a music station, and we started talking. Elijah told me that he was from a forest in northern California. He and his guides lived there for some time before eventually settling here. They were much older than most guides when they received the calling to find him. Sadly, that meant that they had passed away by now. His mom passed first, and he and his dad took her to a forest in the Canadian Rockies and buried her deep within it.

When his dad passed, Elijah brought his ashes to his mother's location and buried them at the roots of the tree she had become. While he was visiting her, he placed his hand upon her bark to give her a growth boost. To his amazement and delight, she remembered him and was so happy to see him. Elijah confided in me that this was the first and last time in his adult life that he wept like a small child.

He also had a very close relationship with his guides and viewed them more as parents. He began massaging my feet and told me what it was like in California and the Canadian Rockies, as I had never left our immediate area. I told him about my desire to one day visit my Mother

Tree and how I hoped she would be proud of me. He assured me that she would be.

His hands made their way to my calves as I told him about school and what I wanted to do with my major once I finished. He had graduated a few years earlier with a degree in environmental law and was now working at a nonprofit firm, taking as many pro bono cases as his expenses allowed. I was in awe. Elijah was the first real, grown-up man I had dated. He asked questions about my recycling business as his hands massaged my thighs.

I told him all about the events we sponsored and the companies we were able to get on board. He agreed that the university asking us to help out with homecoming week was a huge win and a great sign. I told him about my obsession with mythology, and he laughed. We talked about the community garden that I helped set up, and he told me about the tree planting ceremony that he officiated. I snuggled closer to him and wished I had a fireplace. My face was pressed against his neck, and I could smell his musky cologne. It reminded me of the taste in the forest air earlier in the evening, and I wanted to know if his neck would taste as good as it smelled.

I kissed his neck, and his hand froze for a moment. He finally continued the cadence he was massaging into my thigh. I parted my lips and took a taste of his neck. It was similar to the forest air, but with an alcohol undertone from the cologne. He removed one hand from my leg and began playing with my hair. I moved my mouth to his ear and put one hand on his chest. He grabbed my chin and pulled my mouth to his. As our mouths moved together, I repositioned myself so I was sitting on his lap. It quickly became apparent that he was ready to go all the way, and I had to agree.

While I hadn't planned on this happening when I agreed to let him stay over, and I was pretty sure he hadn't either, it felt right. We hadn't been close friends, or even run in the same circles, but we'd known each other for quite some time. I wasn't the type to sleep with someone on the first date, but this didn't feel like a first date. And I was pretty sure I wouldn't have been able to stop myself even if I wanted to.

My body was acting of its own accord. Arching itself in ways I didn't even know was possible, and pressing myself against his body in a way that I was too reserved to do. Even my voice betrayed me, letting out moans and sighs that I didn't give it permission to.

Elijah seemed to enjoy it, and my body gave him more. It longed for this kind of touch so badly that my hands involuntarily removed his shirt and undid his pants. I lifted myself off him long enough for him to remove mine, and my treacherous hands took off my own shirt.

My chest pressed itself into his face as he fiddled with the clasp of my bra. Once he removed it, he carried me the two feet to my bed and crawled on top of me. He kissed my neck and entered my body as soon as he could.

He was bigger than Edgar had been, and so it hurt worse than I thought it would. Elijah saw my face tense and moved more slowly. As time went on, the pain subsided, and my body took over again. I was moaning loudly, my legs wrapped around his waist. He pushed harder, and I dug my nails into his back in pleasure. If I had been with Edgar, he would have been done by now.

Elijah was a mature man who knew how to pace himself. He worshipped my body as he slowly moved in and out of it. Occasionally, he would have quick bursts of fast thrusts until I couldn't take it anymore and I thought my mind would explode.

He flipped us over and admired his view. I looked down at his sweaty body and found myself even more turned on and sexually charged. I closed my eyes and let my body completely take over. I arched my back and lifted myself up and down. I felt my hands grab my breasts, and they were quickly joined by his.

He put an arm around my waist and pulled me into him where he kissed me sloppily. He grabbed hold of my hair and gently pulled my head back to expose my neck. He kissed it and took over the hard work while I just enjoyed the feel of him inside me. Not long after I gave control to him, I reached my climax and cried out louder than I ever had. The explosion was so intense and so powerful that I felt I might melt right into him. I begged him not to stop, but that proved irresistible, and he quickly joined me in ecstasy.

Though the deed was done, I stayed on top of him. I laid against his warm, toned body and willed myself not to melt. He kissed my hair and touched my body in sensitive places. Eventually, I rolled off him so he could clean up.

I expected him to grab his boxer briefs when he stood, but he did not. He was a confident man and strolled to the bathroom naked. When he returned, I admired him. "I swear, I don't usually sleep with someone on the first date," I told him, as he crawled back into the bed.

He laughed softly. "We are two grown adults. There's no time table for when our first time together should be." He thought for a moment. "You don't regret it, do you?"

"Absolutely not. It was amazing. If I weren't so tired, I'd probably vote for a round two."

He smiled and pulled me into him. "Maybe in the morning then."

We talked some more until we fell asleep. The last thing I remember hearing was his voice telling me about when his guides met him at his Mother Tree.

I woke up when Owen knocked on the door. Elijah was still sound asleep next to me. I pulled on my underwear and his shirt before answering the door.

"Oh," he said. "What do we have here?" He looked at the shirt I was wearing and then over my head at Elijah sleeping in the bed. "I see you thoroughly enjoyed your company last night."

"I sure did," I told him, as I took one of the coffees from his hands.

"Maybe I should go wait at Garrett's while you get ready. I don't want to wake him up and have him think I'm an attacker or something."

I groaned. "I don't want to see Garrett until I absolutely have to."

"Don't worry about him," Owen told me." I explained everything, and he isn't mad at you anymore. He does, however, hate Emma even more, which will make things tricky once I get her back."

"I don't know how you can love her like you do."

"In sickness and in health. Drama is her sickness," he explained.

"Owen, that's for married people."

"Potato, potahto," he said and then walked away.

I closed the door and crawled back into bed. I kissed Elijah's ear and neck. "Eli, wake up."

"Is it time for round two already?" he asked sleepily. Then, with surprising strength for being half awake, he pulled me onto him.

"No. Owen's waiting for me to go work on that petition. I just wanted to let you know so you wouldn't freak out when I wasn't here when you woke up."

"Oh. Okay. Do you want me to leave?"

"No. Stay and sleep. You must be exhausted after last night. Just make sure you lock the door when you leave. I don't know how long I'll be gone."

He kissed my lips and turned on his side. He was back asleep within moments.

I took a shower and dressed as fast as I could. I wanted to crawl back into bed every time I glanced over at Elijah. He looked so cozy and warm. I wanted to pin myself under his arm and stay there forever. Instead, I headed to Garrett's apartment to pick up Owen.

Garrett was acting normal, as Owen had promised. It was as though last night had never happened. He joined us for breakfast and eventually decided to help us get signatures for the petition. I was happy that he still wanted to spend time with me and that it wasn't awkward.

As we entered a dorm hall, Garrett asked, "What is this petition for anyway?"

"A developer wants to cut down an old growth forest just outside of town to build a strip mall," Owen explained.

"What? That's ridiculous. Why do we need another strip mall when half of the existing ones are mostly vacant?"

I smiled at him. "That's why we have a petition. Now, you two go on the all girls floors and flirt your way to signatures, and I'll go on the boys' floor."

"I don't think you should go alone, Ella," Owen said.

I rolled my eyes, but then Garrett agreed. "Yeah, a beautiful girl wandering the halls of a testosterone fueled floor alone probably isn't a good idea."

"Fine. Then, Owen can come with me. Garrett will do better getting the girls to sign anyway," I teased.

Garrett laughed at Owen, and we made our way up the stairs. Garrett exited on the first girls' floor, and Owen and I continued up to the boys' floor.

"So, you and Elijah got serious pretty quickly," Owen said.

"Don't judge. It just happened. I couldn't control myself."

Owen laughed. "Are you telling me that a Nymph succumbed to sex against her will? You know how stereotypical that sounds?"

We reached the right floor and exited the stairwell.

"I know, but I don't know how else to describe it. We just connected, and it felt right, and my body took over."

"Whoa. That's enough out of you. I don't need to hear the details."

"Sorry," I said sheepishly.

By the time we finished collecting signatures from the boys, we were surprised to see Garrett waiting for us outside the building. He was smoking a cigarette with a beautiful girl who had to have been a freshman. He spotted us and headed our way.

"Call me!" she yelled after him.

He waved and winked. She giggled.

"Garrett, you know she's illegal, right? There's no way she's eighteen," I said.

"I know," he said. "It's a shame, really." He took a handful of papers out of his pocket and threw them in the trash.

"Were those what I think they were?" I asked.

"Oh my God, Ella. You're too much! Yes, it was paper. It could have been recycled, but I had to get them out of my pocket while I was still thinking with my brain."

Owen laughed.

"That's not what I meant. Were those all phone numbers?"

"What? Oh. Yeah, they were. But as you said, half of that building isn't legal, and the other half is barely. I don't want to tempt myself."

"That's ridiculous," I said.

"That's awesome," Owen countered, high-fiving Garrett.

We continued on to the other dormitories on campus and some of the nearby apartment complexes. It was after dark when we finally filled our clipboards with signatures.

"I can't believe we got one thousand signatures in a day!" Owen exclaimed.

"I told you campus was the way to go. Students are always more willing to answer their doors."

"You were right, Ella. You were right."

I beamed. "I usually am."

"Well, I'm going to drop these off at my place and grab my stuff. I'll be by in a few hours," Owen told me.

"Sure. Here, let me give you a key in case I fall asleep," I said, removing my spare from its ring. I looked at Garrett uneasily.

"Don't worry. I told him all about our arrangement that Armeta is insisting on."

Garrett laughed. "It's one of the silliest things I ever heard. She's having dreams that someone is going to break into your place, so she's making Owen stay with you."

"Yeah. Pretty silly," Owen agreed.

After Owen headed to his place, Garrett and I started towards ours. "So, do you want to go get dinner or a drink or something?" Garrett asked.

"Nah, I'm pretty beat. I think I'm just gonna go take a hot bubble bath and crawl into bed," I told him.

He walked me to my door where I told him goodnight and went inside before he could respond. I found a note on my counter from Elijah. It promised me he would be back tomorrow afternoon. I smiled and put it in my recycle bin.

Just as I had told Garrett I would, I drew a hot bubble bath. I lit about a dozen candles and arranged them around my bathroom. Some were on the seat of the toilet, some on the edge of the sink, some on the floor, and whatever was left, I placed on the edge of the tub. I walked into the living room and turned the stereo on to a classical station before stripping down and submerging myself in the bubbles. I ended up falling asleep in the tub and woke up just before midnight. My fingers and toes were wrinkly, and the water had grown fairly cold. I pulled my robe on and found Owen passed out on the couch. I pulled on some pajamas and crawled into bed.

CHAPTER 10

I stumbled over a large root protruding from the ground. After regaining my footing, I continued on my way. It was urgent that I get to where I was going, but the forest's undergrowth seemed thicker than usual. It was as though the forest itself wanted to prevent me from reaching my destination.

When I finally came upon my Mother Tree, I was relieved that she was still standing. I saw a new wound in her bark, higher up than the previous one. I raised my hand to her and wished I could reach the gash. Suddenly, I was getting taller, but I was not growing, rather the moss under my feet was. It lifted me up higher and higher until I could reach her wound.

It was fresh, sap still seeping out. I looked around for the culprit, but there was no one around. I placed both hands on her bark and sent her every last drop of energy I had. This was not the time to be conservative. Someone was inflicting damage on my Mother Tree, and I had to stop it.

As my energy drained, my Mother Tree began to heal quicker than I had ever seen a tree heal. She sent me images that I did not understand. There was a deer eating leaves off one of her neighbors. It dropped suddenly, and I saw an arrow sticking out of its chest. Then, there was someone walking around the forest, examining each tree, but I couldn't make out who it was. Next, she showed me the first wound being made. All I saw was the hand of the person who did it to her. After that, I saw a man staring at her. I couldn't see his face, but he looked to be of average height and had shaggy light brown hair that kept falling into his face.

Before long, the moss began returning to its normal size since it didn't have any more energy to draw from me. I kept my hands on her bark as I was lowered back to the ground. I could tell I would pass out, but I still did not stop the energy transfer. When I eventually passed out, I saw an image of the man slicing my Mother Tree open again and stealing her sap.

As I was adrift in blackness, I suddenly felt as though the Earth was going to open up beneath me. Surely, there

was an earthquake rumbling the forest. Then, I heard my
name.

"Ella! Ella, wake up! Ella!"

I felt something tugging at my arms and legs, then it
felt almost like snakes were slithering over my body.
When I woke up, Owen was in my face.

"Ella! Are you okay?" He sounded panicked.

"I'm fine. I was just sleeping." I didn't understand his
urgency.

"Just sleeping? Your vines right here," he pointed
next to my bed, "had themselves wrapped around your
arms and legs!"

"That's not possible. They aren't long enough," I told
him.

"Then, they grew. I swear to you, Ella. They were
wrapped around you, and you looked like you were
having a seizure."

I sat up and looked at my vines. They were indeed
longer than before, but not enough to reach me. Yet, I
had red marks up and down my arms and legs. "That's so
weird."

"I've never heard of plants growing without a touch. And definitely not in your sleep!" Owen was practically yelling.

"Me either. Let's keep this to ourselves, okay? I don't want to worry my parents more than they already are," I told him.

"Ella, this is something to worry about. You should tell them."

"No, Owen. They are freaked out enough."

"Then, at least tell the Elders."

"They'll just tell my parents! And everyone else. Then, I'll be even more of a leper. It stays between us. Promise me."

Owen sighed. "Fine, I promise. But I think you should move your plants farther away from your bed."

"Fine," I agreed.

Owen turned out the lights and went back to the couch.

I looked at the clock. It was very early morning, before I would normally wake up. While I felt completely exhausted, I knew there was no way I would be able to sleep. It wouldn't be fair to Owen to stay up and keep him awake, so I decided to start my day early.

By the time I emerged from the shower, Owen was fast asleep.

I got dressed and headed out the door. The birds were singing as though the sun couldn't rise without their help. The sky was a breathtaking pink-orange when the bus pulled up to the stop. I got on and rode it to the local women's shelter. I wished I could still hear the sounds of nature. This hour of the morning was always so peaceful. Instead, I had to settle for watching the sky. It became more orange before it started to become infused with a beautiful pale periwinkle. Eventually, the orange faded away at the horizon, and the sun was shining in a purely blue canvas. Shortly thereafter, the bus came to a stop a few minutes' walk from the shelter.

As I was walking alone I remembered that I wasn't supposed to go anywhere by myself. I was still mad at Emma, so I didn't want her to join me. And if I told Elijah or Owen where I was, they would insist on coming with me, but no men were allowed at the shelter. I settled on texting Garrett where I was.

He didn't know exactly why Owen was staying with me. We had played it off as Armeta being silly, which I did think she was a little. Since he didn't know I was in possible immediate danger, he'd see no reason to chase after me. He also probably wouldn't talk to Owen for a few more hours, by which time I'd be headed back home anyway.

I stopped in front of an unmarked building that looked like offices. When I went inside, I was greeted by a woman at the reception desk who had me sign in, even though she knew who I was. She pushed a button that unlocked the door so that I could enter the shelter.

The hallway was brightly painted with a beautiful purple. Before I started coming here, everything was white and beige and incredibly depressing. I thought that if you made things brighter or more vibrant, the residents would feel more alive, and it would help their healing process, so I helped them redecorate.

When I rounded the corner, I came to the living room. The only women up at this hour were those with small children. A few of them still showed signs of the abuse they had fled. Others had been here long enough for the bruising to fade. One of the kids saw me first.

"Ella!" She came running over to me and hugged my leg.

"Hi, Hilary. I see you're feeling better." I smiled at her warmly and hugged her back as best I could. The last time I was here, she had a bruise on her left cheekbone and barely spoke.

Hilary beamed. "Yup! My face doesn't hurt anymore, and Miss Mary has been helping me feel better in here," she pointed at her head, "and in here," she finished, as she pointed to her heart.

"Well, that's awesome!" I told her. "I'll have to give Miss Mary a big thank you when I see her."

Miss Mary was actually Dr. Mary Goldenstein. She was the child psychologist that volunteered here three days a week.

Hilary's mom approached us. "Hilary, let's not take up all of Miss Ella's time. I'm sure she came here to do something important."

I smiled. I was happy to see that all of her bruising had faded as well. "Good morning, Regina. Looks like you're feeling better too."

Regina looked down at her daughter, who ran off to play with some toys. "Mostly. Having Hilary doing so well is really helping."

"I'm so glad to hear. She really seems to be coping well."

"Yeah. Sometimes, she cries for her daddy to come get us. I don't know how to tell her that if Daddy never left in the first place, we probably wouldn't be here."

"As long as she isn't crying for Josh, you know she hasn't become conditioned to the abuse, and that is always a great sign."

Josh was Regina's long-term boyfriend. They were together for about half of Hilary's life, most of which he spent hitting them. When Regina came home from work one day to find Hilary beaten and unconscious, she finally realized she had to get herself and her daughter out of there.

While Hilary was at the hospital, Regina went back to the house to get some of their things. Josh was supposed to be at work, but he came home early, bottle of liquor in hand. When he realized what was happening, he got a few more hits in. Luckily for Regina, he was so drunk at that point that he ended up passing out. She was able to get some of Hilary's favorite toys and books and the family albums from before her husband left. She hasn't looked back since.

"I can't tell you how much your visits mean to her, Ella. To all the kids."

I spent the next several hours talking to the women about what supplies they needed most and what the kids missed most from home. When lunchtime came around, I helped serve the food and cleaned up once everyone was finished. At this point, I had felt my phone vibrate about a dozen times. Clearly, Owen had woken up. Once the kitchen and dining hall were spotless, I said my goodbyes and promised I'd be back soon.

When I got on the bus, I checked my phone. There were texts from Owen and Garrett and a voicemail from Owen. The voicemail was from before he talked to Garrett and didn't know what had happened to me. I was genuinely flattered at how panicked he sounded. I replied to both of them that I was on my way home. Only Owen responded, telling me that Elijah was over, waiting for me to return. This news made me happier than I had expected. I wondered why Garrett didn't respond, but I assumed it was because he didn't know that a bus ride could be dangerous for me these days.

When the bus reached my stop, Austin got on. "Oh, hi, Austin. How have you been?" I asked, as I walked toward him, headed for the door.

Austin looked excited to see me. "Fine."

There he went again with his short, antisocial answers. "Did you pick a topic for the term paper?"

"Uh, yeah. Nymphs," he responded.

I forced a laugh. "Figures a guy would be the one to pick Nymphs," I teased. "I went with Sirens." I was going to continue, but the bus driver was giving me a dirty look. "I guess we'll catch up later."

"Yeah," he said and then found his way to the back of the bus.

I walked to my building and found Owen pacing outside. "Jesus, Ella. You gave me a heart attack!"

"Breathe, Owen. I wanted to go see the women at the shelter so I could figure out what they needed. I plan on setting up a donation booth at the Relay for Life that's coming up."

"If something would have happened to you, your parents would never forgive me. What if you're being followed? You could have been kidnapped right off the bus!"

I laughed as we walked into the building. "Wow. Now, I can sort of get how you and Emma click. You can be just as dramatic as her!"

He gave me a look as we climbed the stairs. "Just don't do that again. Even if I can't go into the shelter, I can still ride the bus with you."

"Men aren't supposed to know the location of the shelter. That would make me a terrible volunteer if I led one right to it."

We exited the stairwell and headed for my door.

"It's me, Ella. You know I'd never hit anyone. No woman is going to have to shack up there to avoid me. And I sure as hell wouldn't let anyone else know where it is."

"I wouldn't have thought Arthur was the abusive type, either, but he sure looked ready to hit Emma yesterday," I commented.

"He did what?" Owen was furious.

"Again, with the flair for drama," I said, as we walked into my apartment. "Emma beat him to it. She slapped him across the face so hard she left a handprint."

Owen looked proud and pissed at the same time. It was an odd combination.

"It's true, man," Elijah said. "I was there. It was great." He walked over to me and gave me a hug. "You gave us a scare, Ella."

"Not you too! I was fine. I walked straight to the bus, straight to the very secure shelter, then straight back again."

"Did you forget I was coming over?"

"Of course not. I just couldn't fall back asleep early this morning, and I had been meaning to get out to the shelter, so I seized the opportunity to go."

Elijah furrowed his brow in concern. "What woke you up?"

I saw Owen's eyes widen with expectation. "Owen was snoring."

"I do not snore!" he exclaimed.

"Yes, you do. You just don't hear it because you're sleeping."

He started to protest again, but I elbowed him in the ribs slyly. "I'm starving. Do you guys want some lunch?"

They did, so I set to work cooking some fish and rice. Instead of helping me, they turned on the TV and found something that held their attention. After we ate, I kicked Owen out so I could have some alone time with Elijah.

We laid down on the bed, and I told him about my visit and what a little trooper Hilary was. He suggested that I post flyers all around campus and in the neighboring community about the Relay donation drive as well as set a bin up at my office with a big sign in the window. "That way, people walking by will see it and hopefully bring stuff in."

"That's a great idea, Eli."

"Eli?"

I chuckled. "Just something I'm trying out. You don't like it?"

"No, I like it just fine. I actually just had a dream the other night that you called me that."

I wanted to ask him if he ever dreamed about his Mother Tree and if it felt as real as it did for me. But I knew I probably shouldn't. "That wasn't a dream. I called you Eli when I woke you up to tell you I was leaving."

"Are you sure?" He was skeptical.

"As sure as I am that I want you to kiss me right now," I told him.

Without comment, he pulled me on top of him and kissed me. It wasn't as hot and heavy as the other night, but it still had a fire to it. We kissed for a few minutes more before I moved to his side and cuddled up to him. He started playing with my hair, and I fell asleep.

I heard the TV going when I woke up. "Eli?"

"Nope. Just me. He left hours ago." It was Owen.

"Hours? What time is it?" I looked at my clock. I had slept the day away. "Crap! I got homework due tomorrow!"

Owen laughed and turned his attention back to the TV. He was watching a program about the ancient forests of Michigan, most of which had been logged to death.

I found my book bag and set it on one of the chairs at the counter. For the next three hours, I worked on biology and chemistry homework. When I pulled my attention away from my notebook, I saw that Owen had fallen asleep. I turned the TV off and moved my plants away from my bed before changing into pajamas. I was happy to find that I fell into a dreamless sleep.

The next day, I found myself dreading my Mythology class. I hated not looking forward to it because it was always my favorite, but I didn't know if Brandon would be awkward.

When I got into the classroom I found Austin sitting in the seat next to mine. It was a pretty bold move for him based on our previous encounters. I walked over and sat down.

"So, Sirens, huh?" he started.

"Yeah. Brandon wanted to hear my unique take on them. He doesn't think I'll find any text to back up my theory."

"But you think you will?"

"I'm sure I will."

"If you need any help tracking information down, let me know," Austin offered.

I wondered if he had taken an anti-anxiety pill today. "Thanks, but I'm sure I'll be fine."

"Well, then, if you want company. Maybe we could research together."

I wasn't sure, but it sounded like he was trying to set up a date. I found myself wondering if this was the same Austin I had been randomly bumping into. In case that was his intent, I thought I should let Elijah's existence be known.

"Thanks, Austin, but I'm pretty sure my boyfriend will keep me company."

"Oh, that hu... hunky looking brunette dude with the beard that's always following you around?" Austin blushed.

"No. Not him. He's just a friend. You think he's hunky?" I raised an eyebrow at him.

"Uh, no. I have just heard others, uh, refer to him that way."

Before I could respond, Brandon came into the room. He looked around and smiled when he saw me. That was a good sign. He immediately jumped into his lecture about *The Odyssey* right where he left off. I chose not to participate much, but plenty of other students filled the void. When he dismissed us, I approached him.

"I decided on Sirens. Is that okay?"

"I had a feeling you'd go that way. When Kasandra asked for the topic, I told her it was already taken."

"That was very sweet of you."

"Just trying to be a good teacher," he responded, and I realized things were, indeed, awkward like I thought they would be.

"Brandon, can we please just pretend like that never happened?"

He blushed a little and looked around to make sure no one was in listening distance. "I'm sorry, Ella. I don't think I can push it out of my mind. It was pretty amazing. But I can promise I won't ever bring it up. If you decide that getting involved isn't a bad idea, let me know, and I'll be on board. But I won't pursue it again. I don't want you to feel weird around me, okay?"

I didn't have the heart to tell him that I had a boyfriend now and it would probably never happen. "Okay."

Done with classes for the day, I headed home. There was a box in the hallway addressed to me when I got there. When I got inside, I opened it and discovered a bouquet of sunflowers. I inhaled their fragrance and put them in a vase. I was about to call Elijah to thank him when I saw the note.

> *Ella,*
>
> *Please forgive me. You have to know I was just trying to help you in my own way. I'm sorry if I messed your business up.*
> *Always your sister,*
> *Emma*

While the sentiment was sweet, I wasn't ready to forgive her.

Over the next several days, more and more flowers were delivered to my apartment. When I still didn't respond, she started sending them to the office. Garrett thought it was hilarious and applauded me for not giving in at first. Eventually, though, they worked their charm on him.

"Maybe you should forgive her, Ella," he told me, as he brought a bouquet of mums into my office.

"Traitor." I glared at him.

"She's obviously sorry. And based on her cards, I dare say, she did mean well."

"Mean well? Who are you, and what have you done with Garrett? Did you forget what she did? She intentionally hurt you. For *fun*. I don't care what her cards say. She did it for her amusement."

"You should at least call her," he said.

"No. I'm still mad at her. Things still aren't the same between you and me. I miss how it used to be, and it's her fault."

"Ella, she's been sending you flowers and plants for days. She's sorry. She wishes she could take it back."

I opened my mouth to contradict him, but Garrett placed his finger against my lips and hushed me. My heart quickened as I felt an electric pulse flow through my body. It seemed like time stood still for just a moment while I felt the pressure of his finger against my lips. I cursed myself for still letting him make me feel this way.

"Hear me out." When I made no move to interrupt him, he continued. "I would have found out about Elijah eventually. And when that happened, things would have changed. It's one thing to flirt with an unattached friend, even if I did really mean it. But I would have stopped once I knew about Elijah, whether she had told me or if I just stumbled upon it. Especially because I mean it."

I frowned at him and his logic.

"And besides, I am with Bridget now, so that changes our dynamic regardless of your dating status."

I sighed. "I hate when you're right."

"And I hate when you're upset," he told me. He pulled me into a tight, comforting embrace then released me quicker than was usual for him. "Call Emma and forgive her before people start having allergy attacks right before homecoming."

I laughed at this as he walked away and then picked up my phone to call Elijah to cancel our plans for the night. "Yes, I really am going to need the whole night to make up with her."

"What exactly does making up with her entail? Maybe I should come and lend a hand," he teased.

"Eli! You filthy Nymph. Get your head out of the gutter. There will probably be ice cream and crying and her talking my ear off. Not necessarily in that order."

He laughed, which momentarily distracted me. He had such a sexy laugh, and my body was craving his again. We had been taking it slow after jumping into bed together so quickly in the beginning. I reminded myself that I went years without sex before and that this past week was nothing. Then, my mind reminded me that I was single during that drought, and now that I had a boyfriend, it wasn't the same.

"Maybe you should come over and kick Owen out so you can wait up for me," I told him.

He groaned. "You know I'd love to, but I'm working on this really big case, and I can't get distracted right now."

"Hmm. Maybe I'll just have to find another way to distract you then."

He laughed again. "Goodbye, Ella. Good luck tonight."

"Bye, Eli."

After I hung up, I walked over to Garrett's office. "I know homecoming week starts on Monday and there's still a lot of prep work to be done, but do you think you could handle it? I want to head over to Emma's before I change my mind."

"Sure thing. But didn't Owen say that Armeta wanted someone to walk with you wherever you go?"

I rolled my eyes. "It's just a few blocks from here, and you know where I'm going. I'll be fine."

"Okay, but if for some reason Armeta's irrational fears come true, I'm not taking the fall."

I playfully smacked him on the arm and went on my way.

CHAPTER 11

It was raining out, and I had forgotten my umbrella. Rather than rush to Emma's to avoid the rain, though, I took my time. It was unseasonably warm, and I took the time to enjoy the feel of the rain falling down on me. A drop landed on my eyelashes, and they clumped together, creating a blurry dark spot in my vision. I watched as the grass greedily drank up the rain and threatened to grow some more. Birds took cover in the tree branches, and squirrels hurried about their business. A car drove by and splashed a large puddle of water onto the sidewalk ahead of me. I may have been enjoying the rain, but I was glad that missed me.

I arrived at Emma's, dripping wet, and knocked on the door. A man answered, and I was so surprised that it took me a moment to realize it was Austin.

I looked at the number on the door. "Do I have the wrong building?" I asked.

He opened his mouth to speak, but Emma's voice came from further inside. "Who is it?"

Austin and I looked at each other dumbfounded. He was wearing a green button-down shirt and khaki pants, a far cry from his usual dingy attire. Annoyed that no one answered her, Emma came walking up the hallway.

When she saw it was me, she ran the last few steps and squeezed past Austin to hug me tight. "Ella! Oh, thank you, Ella! I've missed you so much!"

My arms wrapped around her like a reflex.

"What happened to you?" she asked. "You're soaked!"

Austin stepped aside as she pulled me in. Her roommate didn't appear to be home, and the table was set for two, but the food had already been eaten.

"Is Darla here?" I asked, eyeing the plates.

"No," Emma responded. "She went home for the weekend. I don't think she's coming back until tomorrow."

I again stared at Austin like an idiot. He gave me a sheepish smile. "I was hoping we could talk," I told Emma. "Just the two of us."

"Oh, sure thing. I'll call you later, Austin, okay?" she said.

He nodded, and I about fell over when Emma kissed him before he left.

Once the door was closed, I whirled on her. "You and Austin?"

She looked confused for a moment. "Oh, that's right. He saw your picture in my room and told me you guys had a class together."

"Yeah, he sits next to me in Mythology. How long have you been dating?"

"I ran into him that night at the bar after you stormed off. He saw how upset I was and wanted to comfort me."

I ignored the accusation that I 'stormed off' and concentrated on the important points. "And you started dating?"

"Well, I brought him back to my place because I wanted to get laid, and when I woke up in the morning, I realized I couldn't let him go."

"He must be damn good in bed," I commented.

"Why do you say that?"

I was surprised she didn't take it to mean I wanted details. "He's a human, Emma."

"So?" she asked, nonchalantly.

"So? A human. As in, not a Nymph. Or a Fairy. You never date humans. I know you've slept with your fair share of them, but you'd never date one."

She shrugged her shoulders. "Humans are people too."

"Seriously?"

"Yeah. But enough about me, what's been going on with you?"

"Really? You want to hear about my life?"

"Of course, Ella, but first, let's get you something dry to change into." She disappeared into her room and came back with a pair of skinny jeans and an oversized pink sweater.

"Well," I started, as I began removing my wet clothes, "Elijah and I are still going strong." Once my clothes were off, I walked over to her sink and rung my shirt out before hanging it over a dining chair.

"Did you have sex yet?"

"Actually, we did. Just once."

"Just once? Why? Wasn't it any good?"

I pulled on the jeans and idly wondered what Eli would think about the fact that I was just prancing around half naked in front of Emma. "Hell no. It was amazing. He was so tender and attentive." I pulled the sweater over my head and joined her on the couch. "He's like the first real man I've been with. Patient and slow, but hot and crazy too."

Emma pretended to fan herself. "Hot, Ella. I told you that you needed to get laid! But if it was so great, why haven't you done it again?"

I didn't want to tell her the complete reason that would let her know how quickly we jumped into bed, not that she'd judge. Instead, I said, "We've just been really busy. He's working on a major case, and I have been prepping for homecoming week and the Relay for Life. Plus, with Owen living with me, it makes it difficult."

"Maybe you should stay at Elijah's place."

"I already thought of that, but he lives with three of his friends."

Emma winked at me. "Sounds like a good time to me."

I threw one of the couch pillows at her.

We talked for hours. She asked me about my work at the women's shelter and how she could help. She thought it would be a good idea to also set up the bins for homecoming week and even offered to help set them up for each of the upcoming events. We avoided talking about Garrett.

Amazingly, I had to prompt her in order to hear anything about her life. It seemed she and Austin were pretty serious, and she was spending most nights at his place a few buildings over. I felt bad for thinking he tried to ask me out. He had been dating Emma at that point and probably was trying to get us back together. I felt like their relationship also explained his recent confidence boost.

After we talked about everything we possibly could have, I headed home. It was well after midnight, and so I was surprised when I opened the door and saw candles lit all around the room. Owen was nowhere to be seen, and Elijah was sitting on the bed waiting for me.

When I walked in, he put his book down and looked up at me, smiling. "Nice outfit. Twirl around so I can see it from all angles."

I did as he asked, and he whistled while I spun. "They're Emma's," I explained. "I was soaking wet from the rain by the time I got there."

"It looks great on you. It's a shame I have to take them off already." He grabbed my waist and pulled me up against the bed where he lifted my shirt just enough to kiss my stomach.

"I thought we were taking things slower," I said.

"We've waited long enough," he told me.

As I let myself really feel his kisses on my stomach and his hands now grabbing my ass, my body took over. I pulled the sweater off and removed my bra. His mouth traveled higher as his hands unbuttoned my pants.

Once I was fully naked, he laid me on the bed and kissed his way south. I enjoyed the feel of his tongue and let myself go. It wasn't long before I reached my peak, and he stripped naked. Turns out, that wouldn't be my only moment of bliss that night. He truly was a patient man.

When morning came, I did not want to get up. I was content to lay naked in bed with Eli all day.

I reached out to pull him closer to me so that I could feel the heat of his body against mine before falling back asleep. Instead, I found a piece of paper. I squinted my eyes open to read it.

My darling Ella,

I had to go into the office bright and early to finish working on my case. It was difficult to pry myself away from you, but I take solace in knowing we will be together again soon. You looked so content and peaceful that I didn't want to wake you. Owen should be here soon, possibly before you wake.

All of my affections,

Eli

While slightly disappointed, I was left with a feeling of contentment, knowing he was experiencing the same yearning. I lifted my head from my pillow and saw that Owen was sitting at the counter working on homework.

I gathered my sheets around my body and stumbled into the bathroom, mumbling a quick, "Good morning," as I passed him.

After my shower ran cold, I begrudgingly wrapped myself in my favorite fluffy red towel and realized I didn't think to bring any clothes into the bathroom with me. When I opened the door and stepped into the living room, I saw that Owen had ordered pizza and invited Garrett over to eat.

I caught Garrett looking me up and down, dripping wet in my towel before we locked eyes. I wasn't sure which of us blushed worse. He opened his mouth to speak, but nothing came out. I hurried over to my dresser, pulled out the first articles of clothing I could manage, and hightailed it back to the bathroom to dry off and get dressed.

When I came back out into the living space, Garrett had moved so that his back was to the bathroom door. I adjusted the bottom of my pale-yellow sweater and approached the counter. "Any left for me?" I asked.

Owen responded by opening the box and spinning it around to me. I grabbed a slice as he finally spoke, "I have classes this afternoon, so I asked Garrett to come keep you company for a while. I hope you don't mind."

I risked a glance over at Garrett out of the corner of my eye. He seemed to also be trying to avoid eye contact. "Why would I mind?" I asked.

Garrett finally got his voice back. It cracked at first, so he cleared his throat and tried again. "How long are we going to humor Armeta's dream?"

"Great question," I answered. "I think we should have stopped a while ago."

I could tell Owen wanted to yell at me for my cavalier attitude, but with Garrett there, he couldn't without looking like he was crazy. "Aaron called me while you were sleeping. Armeta's had another dream." Owen looked at me for a pointedly long time.

My mouth went dry, realizing what he was saying— another Nymph had gone missing.

Garrett didn't notice the look between us. "She knows they are just dreams, right?"

Owen responded before I could even open my mouth. "Of course she does, but now that there have been two similar dreams so close together, she is extra worried. This time, she dreamed someone mugged you while you were walking alone, so she's asked that we don't let you go anywhere by yourself. If she had it her way, she'd even have someone sitting in your classes with you."

I sighed loudly and threw my arms up in exasperation. "This is getting ridiculous. While I've been blessed with the best guards a girl could ask for, I'm starting to feel like a prisoner."

Suddenly, Garrett stood up and turned his back to Owen, finally facing me for the first time since I emerged from the bathroom dressed. He reached up over his head and bent his arm down as though he was trying to scratch his back. "Hey, Owen, do me a favor? Pull that knife out of my back, would you?"

I rolled my eyes, but apparently, Owen found it to be a fitting reaction and mimed pulling a dagger out of Garrett's back with great difficulty, like it was really wedged in there deep. "You want to get mine?" Owen said, as he turned around pointing at his back with his thumb over his shoulder.

Before Garrett could play along, I grabbed him by the wrists and reiterated, "I said, my guards are the best. It's just frustrating to have zero time to myself."

I realized I was still holding onto Garrett. I caught his eye and then awkwardly dropped his arms as quickly as I could. I thought I saw him smirk in my peripheral vision, but by the time I looked back at him, he was back to eating his pizza, staring at his plate. Eager to change the subject, I asked Owen if he'd heard from Emma recently.

"No, but I'm sure we'll be back together any day now," he responded confidently.

I involuntarily winced. "Maybe don't be too sure about that."

"Why?" he asked. "What do you know?"

"You remember that guy I told you about? The one I saw at the community garden and now he's in my Mythology class too?"

Garrett chimed in, "You mean your stalker?"

"What about him?" Owen asked.

I gave Garrett a quick glare. "Emma's dating him. When I went over to her place yesterday, he answered the door."

"That doesn't mean they're dating, Ella. I answer your door sometimes," Owen retorted.

"And before he left, she kissed him," I added.

Owen's face dropped ever so slightly, for only a moment, before he got his usual confidence back. "I'm not too worried about it. From what you've told me about the guy, he won't be able to handle Emma. She'll realize we're meant to be together, and things will go back to normal."

"I don't understand why you think the two of you are meant to be together. You've broken up, what, half a dozen times?" Garrett stated.

Owen smiled and said, "Just trust me. I don't expect you to understand."

Garrett laughed. "I can't tell if I should be offended."

Once we finished off the pizza, Owen left for class, leaving me alone with Garrett. "Things are going well with that Elijah guy, I take it?" he asked.

"They are going very well," I smiled. "How's Bridget? Do I ever get to meet her?"

"As long as you promise not to scare her into thinking you practice voodoo," Garrett teased, as he poked me in the side.

"I cannot control what people think about me."

He laughed.

"We should go on a double date," I suggested.

"Do you really think that's a good idea?" he asked.

"Why wouldn't it be? We are best friends and very involved in each other's lives. Our partners need to get comfortable with us," I said, pointing between me and him.

"Yeah, I guess. What about tomorrow night?"

I pretended to think. I already knew tomorrow was no good as we had a Gathering to go to.

"I don't think tomorrow works. How about the night after?"

"Sure. What's going on tomorrow night?" he asked.

"I'm going to Emma's to work on some homework," I lied. I knew there was no chance he'd come looking for me there, so I was in no danger of being caught in a lie. "I've got class in fifteen minutes. I suppose you're going to walk me there?"

"I had better, considering you have a stalker out there."

I rolled my eyes and shook my head.

"Which class? Maybe I'll sit in with you too. That way you can tell your parents I listened," he smiled.

"Biology. Then, I head to Chemistry after that, then straight to Mythology."

"I should definitely sit through your Mythology class with you. Keep an eye on that teacher of yours," Garrett said.

I felt my stomach tie into a knot. "Please don't. It's bad enough you're walking me to classes."

Garrett put his hands to his heart and staggered backward, as though he had suffered a major insult.

"You know what I mean!" I said, as I playfully slapped his hands away from his chest.

I gathered my things and let Garrett walk me to class. He kept his distance as though he was trying to make sure our hands didn't bump into each other. While I respected him for attempting to put up some boundaries out of respect for my relationship with Eli, part of me was a little sad. I couldn't help but feel that it had more to do with his expressing how he felt about me and me turning him down. Things were changing between us, and I could only hope it would be temporary.

We walked the entire way in silence. When we arrived at the building, he insisted on walking me all the way to the classroom door. As he turned around to walk away, I couldn't help it anymore. I grabbed his hand and pulled him back into a hug. I worried for a split second that he wouldn't hug me back, but he did.

"I'll see you right here in an hour to walk you to your next class," he said, as he made his escape.

As promised, Garrett was waiting for me at the end of class to walk me to Chemistry. And when Chemistry was over, he was waiting for me outside the door with a coffee.

When we got to my Mythology class, I walked into the classroom and found Austin sitting next to my seat again. He still looked like Emma had been dressing him, wearing khaki pants with a purple polo shirt and his hair pulled back into a man-bun. As soon as I sat down, he was leaning toward me.

"I hope it wasn't weird seeing me at your friend's house," he said.

"Not at all. I was just surprised. I didn't realize you two had even met," I told him.

"Did you start on your term paper at all? My offer to help still stands. We could meet at Emma's place later tonight. I'm sure she wouldn't mind," he told me.

I was pretty sure she *would* mind. "Thanks. I haven't even started on it yet. Maybe after I make some progress, we can make plans to meet at Emma's and peer review each other's papers," I suggested.

"When do you think that will be?"

I didn't understand why he seemed to be in such a rush. "It isn't due until near the end of term, so it'll probably be sometime in November."

He seemed disappointed. "Oh. Okay. If you want to meet up sooner, let me know."

Before I could respond, Brandon walked into the room, calling the class to attention. He made his usual scan of the room and smiled when he saw me. I smiled back. If only he hadn't come onto me, we could probably be friends after the semester was over and I would no longer have him as a teacher.

"Today, we put *The Odyssey* behind us and shift our focus to Nymphs," Brandon announced.

I blushed the slightest bit and thought I saw Austin turn his head toward me out of the corner of my eye.

"Before we get into it, can anyone tell me the difference between Naiads, Oreads, and Dryads?" When no one volunteered, he made direct eye contact with me. "Anyone?"

I was pretty sure the pink in my cheeks darkened.

"Ella? Any perspectives?"

I took a deep breath and swallowed. I reminded myself it was no different than when I would provide some real histories of other creatures disguised as alternate possibilities.

"Quite frankly, I'm a little disappointed you think Nymphs would be categorized as such. The elements of Nature all work together, so wouldn't it make more sense if Nymphs as a people were connected to all elements? I'll bet you even hold to the sexist belief that all Nymphs are female," I teased.

A few people turned to look at me, and I tried not to let it bother me. It never bothered me for any other topics in this class, so it shouldn't for this. Austin was downright staring at me. Even after I looked back at him, he didn't look away, probably shocked that I just implied our teacher was sexist.

"On the contrary, I happen to think there would be both male and female Nymphs to sustain the population. And an interesting comment on the subspecies. I hadn't thought of it that way before. It makes sense. Alas, I have to cover all three sub-species regardless of what our resident expert has to say." He smiled warmly at me, so as to convey I hadn't offended him, before addressing the rest of the class. "Any other comments before we dig in?"

Austin raised his hand.

Brandon pointed at him. "Yes? You, next to the opinionated girl."

Austin cleared his throat. "Who's to say Nymphs are born in the same way as humans?"

My heart started thumping in my chest.

"Okay, if not born how humans are, then how would they repopulate?"

Austin took a glance over at me, and I tried to compose my face.

He smirked and said, "Beats me," and the class laughed.

As Brandon continued teaching everyone inaccurate information, I nudged Austin with my elbow and whispered, "Good one."

I decided not to speak up for the rest of class. When Brandon dismissed us, Austin offered to walk me home. He said he was going that way anyway since he was headed to Emma's. I thanked him and told him I was meeting a friend. As we walked through the doors, Garrett spotted us. He hooked me by the arm and started walking me away from Austin.

"Garrett, I live that way," I said, pointing behind us.

"We are going the long way. I don't like that guy. I don't want him near you," he said.

"What guy?" I asked. "Austin? He's harmless."

"I get a weird vibe. We are going the long way, and that's that." He seemed to notice our arms were still linked together and pulled away.

"You are officially never allowed to give Armeta a hard time about worrying over her dreams," I told him.

He merely smirked back at me.

We walked back to my place in silence. *Great. More silence between us.* When we got there, we found Owen unlocking the door to my apartment, so Garrett said quick goodbyes before hurrying back to the stairwell.

"What was that about?" Owen asked.

"You," I responded.

"Me? What did I do?" Owen's face fell into a concentrated frown as he pondered this.

"You gave him the bright idea to confess his feelings for me. That, plus him finding out about Eli, things are weird between us now. It sucks, and I blame you."

As soon as he got the door open, I walked past him and straight to bed. I was exhausted. Homework would have to wait.

CHAPTER 12

Not long after I closed my eyes, I found myself standing in front of my Mother Tree. The forest around her was unnaturally dark, and the air felt stale. I looked up at her as I reached out to place my hands upon her bark and offer my energy to her.

Several things happened at once.

I saw flashes of images, same as before. A deer snacking on a nearby tree before being downed by a skilled arrow to the chest, a man cutting into my Mother Tree's bark carefully at first, then a second time with more violence. She bled as he collected her sap. I was frustrated that I still couldn't see his face.

Then, I saw some new images.

A couple of squirrels chasing each other up a tree. A cardinal landing on the forest ground a few feet away. After that, I heard the most awful sound. The birds all took off, chattering loudly in protest. In the distance, a twig snapped on the ground as a terrified deer bolted.

The noise was not one of nature. It was man made. Loud and threatening. I didn't recognize what it was until I heard it make contact with my Mother Tree. I felt her extreme pain and opened my eyes to confirm what I had heard. Someone had used a chainsaw to remove one of her lower limbs.

I immediately pushed all my energy out of my body and into my Mother Tree. The ground began shaking beneath my feet, and it felt as though it would swallow me up. I didn't care. Someone disfigured my Mother Tree, and I had to help her.

I felt the wooziness of collapse start to come on, but I closed my eyes and pushed harder. My arms and legs felt constricted as I struggled to push every ounce of my life force into her. My fingers felt like they were on fire with the electricity of the transfer.

As I was losing consciousness, prepared to let the Earth swallow me whole, I opened my eyes and saw the impossible. The gashes in her bark were fully healed, and her limb was well on its way to growing back. Even a fully mature Nymph couldn't have done that. I looked around to see if perhaps someone was there with me, helping me.

I glimpsed someone with sandy brown hair ducking behind a tree in the distance as I finally passed out.

When I woke up, I was back in my room, but it looked like a jungle. My arms and legs still felt constricted, and my heart was pounding. I felt energized and exhausted at the same time. The plants in my room had overgrown more than the last time. They were covering nearly every open space. And they were... glowing. It was faint, but they were definitely radiating.

"Ella?" I heard Owen's voice sounding panicked.

"Is she okay?" This time it sounded like Eli, but he was supposed to be working late. I tried to look toward the sound of his voice but found that I couldn't move my head.

"Ella? Can you hear me?" Owen asked, still with a panic in his voice.

"Yes," I said, but I could barely hear my own voice. It was so quiet.

"Are you okay?" He finally worked his way close enough to position his face above mine. I could see the uncertainty in his eyes.

"Why can't I move?" I asked, again in a voice quieter than it should have been. As my heart pounded in my chest, I swore I saw the plants pulsate in time.

"You need to try and relax."

There was that voice again from near the door. "Eli? Is that you?" I squeaked out.

"Don't try to speak. Just calm down. Listen to the rhythm of my voice. Focus on it, and slow your heart," he responded.

"But what are you doing here? You should be at work." I didn't mean to scold him. I was just so confused. I felt like I was still in a dream. I couldn't get my body to do what I asked of it. My voice wouldn't come out as loud as it was supposed to. My head wouldn't turn. Even my arms and legs felt paralyzed.

"Owen called me. He couldn't wake you up, and your plants were taking over," he explained, keeping his voice calm and smooth. "Has this ever happened before?" he asked.

"No," I said.

Owen furrowed his eyebrows at me, then turned his head toward the door. "Yes, it happened last week, but not this bad. The vines only grew enough to wrap around her arms and legs, and her seizure didn't last as long as it did this time." He looked back at me with an apology in his eyes.

I opened my mouth to complain, but he cut me off.

"Be mad at me all you want, but this is not normal, and I couldn't wake you up this time. I got scared, and I figured you'd rather I call Elijah than your guides."

I tried to shrug my shoulders but couldn't. "Why can't I move?"

"Your plants have you completely wrapped up. They are on tight. I can't get them off. And they are getting longer and tighter," he explained.

As he said this, I realized it had been getting harder to breathe, and I couldn't feel my toes or fingers anymore. He must have seen the terror in my eyes once the realization hit.

"Don't worry." He smiled in an attempt to be reassuring, but he couldn't hide that he was scared too. "Just listen to Elijah's voice. Do what he says."

"Ella, hear me. Close your eyes, and listen to my voice." He was speaking slowly and deliberately. "Focus on the pace. Match your heart to the pace of my voice. Slow it down. That's it, nice and steady. Remember our first night together, when I was giving you a massage. Remember how relaxed you felt. Focus on that."

I did my best to do as he said. I closed my eyes and focused on him. On his voice and his rhythm. I remembered our first night. How it felt to have his hands on me. How I melted into him. I felt the vines loosen their hold. They hadn't retreated yet, but they loosened and stopped throbbing. The pulsing light coming from them was slowing and dimming.

"It's working!" Owen said, attempting to ease the vines off my arms.

"That's it. You're doing great." Eli sounded closer. "Just keep focusing on my voice. Settle your heart, and clear your mind of everything except my voice. I'm coming to you. I'll be there soon. Just let me in, and you'll be okay. We'll get through this, and it'll be okay."

I could hear him getting closer with every word. I tried my best to focus on that. The way I would feel when he finally reached me, and I could feel his body next to mine. The vines loosened more, and I could feel my toes and fingers again. Eli continued speaking in a near trance-like tone. Eventually, he was able to get close enough to put a hand on my foot. The warmth of his touch washed through me, and the vines began retreating faster. I could finally move my head again. I lifted myself up the best I could and opened my eyes so that I could see him.

I was so focused on calming down that I hadn't noticed the vines had already released my upper body and were just lingering on my legs. I propped myself up on my elbows and made eye contact with Eli. He showed no trace of panic, and as his hand traveled over the remaining vines onto open spaces of my skin, I was finally able to release the last of them.

There were still several vines around my bed, making it impossible for me to go to him, but now that they were no longer threatening me, Eli channeled his own energy into them to send them back to their previous sizes. I surveyed the room quickly and saw a few things broken, glass and ceramic shattered on the floor.

As soon as the path cleared, Eli was at my side pulling me up into a hug. "Why didn't you tell anyone the first time this happened?" he asked gently.

"I didn't want to worry anyone with everything else going on."

"Oh, Ella. There are things you don't know," he said. He hugged me again, more tightly this time. He released me from his embrace but made sure to maintain skin to skin contact before continuing. "There are things only the Elders and their understudies know, and this is incredibly important information. They should have shared it with you when they told you about the disappearances from your forest."

Owen looked puzzled. "How do you know they have secret information?"

Eli looked over to Owen without letting me go. "My guides were understudies before they passed. They shared the information with me, hoping I'd be able to take over their studies after they were gone," he explained.

He effortlessly picked me up and moved me to the couch, knowing I'd be too weak to stand, and the three of us sat together while he shared what he knew.

"They didn't tell me everything, but they told me enough to know you need to go to the Elders with this, or at least your parents as they have begun the training. A few centuries ago, when the Nymphs were first venturing beyond the forest, it was foretold that a Nymph would be borne of smoke and power. She would be capable of more than anyone who came before her. It is said she will be a bridge and that she would be able to restore. As she matured, she would not be hindered by touch to channel her energy, and she would have a special connection with the forest."

"And you think this prophesied Nymph is Ella?" Owen asked in slight disbelief.

"Have you ever known anyone to grow plants in their sleep? Without touching them?" Eli responded. Before Owen could comment, he added, "Remember that time in the forest at the Gathering when she showed me the tree she'd been healing? To heal a tree to that degree in such a short amount of time should take a much older, more practiced Nymph. I wrote it off, thinking others must have seen the tree and made offerings as well, even though I did not sense anyone else's energy, because it seemed impossible. And what about how she feels when she connects to the Earth? I was able to feel a small part of it when she rubbed some dirt on me, and let me tell you, I'd never felt anything so powerful before."

"So, now I'm a prophecy?" I asked. "That's not possible. I'm nothing special."

"I know several men who would disagree," Owen stated, then added. "No offense, Elijah."

Eli smiled. "Absolutely none taken. Here's the bad part," he continued. "We can pretty much guarantee now that the person kidnapping women from Ella's forest is in fact looking for her."

I leaned forward, propping my elbows on my knees in front of me and dropped my head in my hands.

"Fuck," Owen said.

"I'm not leaving your side unless a fellow Nymph, who is fully aware of the situation, is with you. We'll talk to the Elders at the Gathering tomorrow to ask for some skilled volunteers to stand watch outside of your classrooms and keep an eye on you when Owen and I are unavailable." Eli was talking more to himself than either of us. "And if it's okay with you, I'd feel more comfortable if I moved in until we figure out who is after you and put an end to all this."

"Fine by me," Owen said, as though it was his permission Eli was seeking.

My head was still hanging down in my hands, but I managed a nod. This was all too much. I felt sick. My life was already complicated enough, and now I had to have a bodyguard around the clock. "Can I at least be left alone if I'm with Emma?" I asked, finally sitting up again.

Eli hesitated.

"I know she doesn't seem like much, but trust me, she is a force to be reckoned with. And even if she's mad at me, she will do everything in her power to protect me," I pleaded.

"It's true," Owen confirmed.

"Fine. You can be left alone if you're with Emma. Let's make sure to bring her into the conversation with the Elder's tomorrow."

"And what about Garrett?" I asked.

"What about him?" Eli responded.

"Can I be free of a bodyguard if I'm with him?

"Ella," Eli started carefully, "I know he cares for you and would protect you if it came down to it, but what chance would he stand against whatever force is trying to hurt you? And he wouldn't know to take it seriously. Doesn't he just think we are humoring Armeta?"

I sighed, knowing he was right. "Then, one of the volunteers will need to become an intern for us. I can't explain a bodyguard at work."

"Yes. Of course. Good idea." Eli nodded.

We sat in silence for a bit while I gathered my strength. Finally, when I felt I could handle it, I told them about my dream. They both listened intently and asked a few questions, mostly trying to help me remember more about the person I thought I saw.

It was sometime after midnight when Owen went home. Eli carried me to bed and helped me undress. He laid down beside me with his bare chest pressing against my back and his hand resting on my hip. After a few minutes, his grip on my hip went slack, and I knew he was asleep. I tried to focus on his breathing and the warmth of his body against mine, hoping it would help me relax into sleep, but it didn't work. I had too much to think about and was so worried my plants would attack me in my sleep again. Eventually, my eyes became too heavy to stay open, and I drifted to sleep as dawn started shining through the window.

When I woke up a few hours later, Eli handed me a coffee and gave me a kiss. He started the shower while I gulped the coffee down greedily. When he came back, he was completely naked. He walked me to the bathroom where he undressed me, and we got into the shower. He helped me wash my hair and my body. When I stumbled back into him, I felt him throb against me.

I spun around and put my arms around his neck and kissed him as deeply as I could. He was surprised at first but quickly returned my passion. I reached my hand down to grab him and guide him inside of me.

When he slid in, he was slow and careful. After a few minutes, he grabbed underneath my thighs and lifted me up, allowing him to penetrate deeper. He pressed me against the shower wall while he moved deeper still. He buried his face in my chest and held my hands above my head. While other orgasms with him had been explosive, this one was more of a slow burn. I let out a soft moan as I felt myself throbbing around him, and shortly thereafter, he moaned through his release as well. A first for him.

He remained inside of me and kissed me everywhere he could reach. He released one of my hands to grab hold of my breast while he kissed the opposite side of my neck just below my ear. I could feel him still pulsing inside me, and it all proved too much. I moaned even louder and orgasmed again.

We remained connected as long as we could, kissing some more. He was still breathing heavily from his climax when he whispered. "I love you, Ella."

Goosebumps raised across my entire body as his breath hit my ear, and my heart exploded when I heard his words. "I love you too," I told him. We went for one more round before rewashing our bodies and stepping back into reality.

After we were dressed, we walked to my class together, hand in hand. When we got to the door, he kissed me, then took his post, sitting next to the door. When I emerged an hour and a half later, he walked me to my next class. After classes were done, we went to his office so he could get some work done and I could do some homework.

It wasn't too far from campus, and it had a very earthy feel, decorated in warm colors with plenty of houseplants. His office held an oak bookcase full of law books, as well as a weathered oak desk with an ergonomic chair and a brown leather loveseat. His walls were adorned with still shots of nature, and the plants in his office were the healthiest and most vibrant in the building. There was a picture of me on his desk that he had taken with his cellphone. He kept it framed near his monitor. Seeing it made me smile at the memory of the moment when he took it. I hadn't realized he framed it for his office.

I found myself in the loveseat, less focused on my homework than usual. I couldn't stop looking up at him. He looked even more devastatingly handsome while he worked. He got up to retrieve a book from the shelf, then sat back down at his desk and opened a drawer. He pulled out a pair of thick framed glasses, put them on, and started scanning the text. I realized I had started holding my breath, and when I let it out, he looked up at me.

"Is something wrong?" he asked with a hint of concern in his voice.

"I didn't know you wore glasses," I commented, raising an eyebrow.

"I try not to advertise it," he said with a smile and started to lift his hand to take them off.

"Just when I thought you couldn't get any sexier," I said coyly.

"Really?" he asked, as his hand reached the frames, ready to pull them off. He changed his mind and left them on.

I smiled at him and then did my best to refocus on my homework. I had already stolen enough of his time to protect me, the least I could do was control myself so that he could try and catch up on his work.

As the afternoon turned into evening, we headed home to prepare for the Gathering. Eli helped me braid the ivy into my hair, and we changed into our traditional garments. We met up with Owen on our way to the bus.

Once we got to the clearing, we tracked down Emma, Aaron, and Armeta and approached the Elders. I let Eli and Owen do most of the talking, nodding my affirmation and only speaking if I absolutely had to.

Owen told them about how he found me the first time, and Eli explained how much wilder it was the second time. I had to explain my dreams to them. Emma stayed surprisingly quiet. She almost seemed bored.

"It's as we suspected," Aaron said to Armeta.

"This doesn't prove she's the Foretold," commented Eugene.

Eli raised his voice in response. "How can you not see it? Too many things are happening for it to be a coincidence!"

My brain finally caught up, and I turned to my parents. "You knew? Why didn't you tell me?" I was slightly outraged.

Armeta reached out for my hand. "We couldn't be sure. We merely suspected. Ever since we answered our call, we could sense there was something special about you. Your connection to your Mother Tree, and then as you got older, you were progressing so much more quickly than you should have been." She gave my hand a little squeeze.

"And then there's your friendship with Garrett," Aaron added.

I let go of Armeta's hand. "What in the world does that mean?"

"It is said the Foretold will develop deep connections with other species, not just her own. That she will bridge the two together and restore balance," Aaron explained.

Eli looked pained but added, "Some believe the Foretold will act as a physical bridge. She won't just develop a deep connection with another species. She will tie herself to it completely and everlastingly."

For what felt like the hundredth time this week, my head was spinning. "Then, there's no way it's me. I'm bonded to you, Eli."

Armeta quickly interjected before anyone else could speak. "Ella, dear, the prophecy is open to interpretation. It doesn't explain what it means to be a bridge, nor does it say what the Foretold will restore. There are many interpretations, and it could be as simple as close friendship."

I started to object, but she stopped me.

"We know you've always been close with Garrett. We aren't sure why you've tried to hide it, but we have always seen past that." She must have seen how miserable I felt because she added, "We are not upset about it, Ella. You are your own spirited self, and it's not for us to judge how you manage your life. Please don't feel bad."

"Is this why you insist from time to time that I bring him over?" I asked.

"We have several reasons, but yes, that is one of them," Aaron answered. "We have been trying to decipher this for some time and thought if we could witness your interactions with an outsider firsthand, it would become clearer. Plus, we do enjoy his company as well."

Eli turned to Olivia. "Please, can we call for volunteers tonight to stand watch over Ella? She'll need a constant companion, and Owen and I aren't enough to cover it. They'll need to be far along in their studies to properly protect her."

"And I'll need someone my age to be an intern," I added.

Olivia looked confused. "An intern? For what?"

Eli explained so that I didn't have to, and to my surprise, Emma volunteered. "I'll do it. I'll be the most inconspicuous one for the job. No one will question my proximity to her," she said.

"It is done," Eugene said. "We will call for volunteers after the opening blessing, but we will not tell them that we believe you are the Foretold. Such a determination cannot be formed lightly. We will only tell them we have very good reason to believe you are the next target, given your Birth Forest."

I found it difficult to dance for the opening blessing once the ceremony started. I was zapped of energy and wasn't looking forward to the stares once the Elders requested bodyguards for me.

Eli stayed close throughout the night. When we went for our traditional post ceremony walk, he held my hand and would not let go. Owen was on my other side and passed the joint to me as soon as he lit it.

I took a short drag, then offered it to Eli while I let the smoke swirl through my lungs. It burned, but it let me know I was still alive while the rest of my body felt numb. He took a small hit and passed it back. I made to pass it to Owen, but he was already pulling a second out of his pocket just for himself. I finished the rest by myself as Eli kept refusing. He wanted to stay alert, he said.

We made it to the tree I'd been helping, and I was glad to see she was almost completely healed. Just one more energy transfer should do it. I lifted my free hand to place my palm upon her bark, but Eli pulled me back. Before I could protest, he raised his free hand and provided the offering for me. He said a few words quietly to the tree while he provided his energy, "Please accept this offering. Take it in and allow it to heal what is injured and sustain what is well." When he stepped back, we could see that this would be the last offering she needed. I thanked him, and we headed back to the clearing.

Emma had already gone, and Owen was hoping to catch her on the bus, so he left without eating. Eli and I filled a plate to share, then found a spot near the fire where we sat and ate. When we were done, he sank to the cool ground with his back leaning against the log. He spread his legs so that I could sit between them and lean back against him. We stayed like that for what felt like hours, just glad to be in each other's presence, watching the fire. Several couples around us were deep in conversation, and a few were engaged in acts of affection. I caught a glimpse of Aaron and Armeta across the fire. Armeta gave me a knowing look, and I could tell she was happy for me that I'd found a partner.

Eventually, I must have fallen asleep because the next thing I knew, I was in Eli's arms, and we were halfway to the bus. I nuzzled my face into his chest and fell back asleep.

CHAPTER 13

The next several weeks were fairly uneventful. With everything going on, I canceled the double date with Garrett. He didn't seem to mind much. He stopped by my place a few times, but Eli was almost always there, so he didn't stick around for long.

It wasn't that Eli wasn't warm and welcoming when Garrett came over, but I think Garrett just felt uncomfortable. Slowly, his visits became less often until it got to the point that I really only saw him at work. He complained a little when he found out I let Emma come on as an intern, but I convinced him that with the large events coming up we needed the extra hands on deck.

Emma was acting strange, though. I guessed the news about the Foretold and finding out there was a very real chance that I was the one the unknown entity was looking for had her nearly as freaked out as me. We barely spoke, and when we did, it was brief. When homecoming week came, she did an amazing job placing bins for the women's shelter donations and socializing with nearly every passerby, letting them know what the bins were for and what sort of items would have the largest impact. Most bins were at least half full by the day of the event. Emma even helped place the recycle bins on event day and helped gather them back up after they'd been emptied the next day.

As time passed, I became used to my new routine. If Owen or Eli weren't home with me, one of the older members of the clan would be sitting in the hallway outside my door. He'd walk me to class and hang out in the hallway nearby, but not close enough to draw attention. The volunteers always wore backpacks and made sure to walk just far enough away that no one would know they were actually walking with me. I was beginning to feel like bait.

The nights Eli stayed with me were always my favorite. Most nights, we stayed in, but occasionally, I got too stir-crazy and convinced him we needed to go out. Tonight, we were headed to my favorite bar for a few drinks—only for me because he didn't think he should be drinking if he was acting as my bodyguard—and some dinner.

When we walked in, I noticed Garrett was there with a woman. They looked fairly cozy together, so I assumed it was Bridget, and I reprimanded myself for feeling jealous about it. Garrett caught me staring at them and waved us over. As we approached, he stood to give me a hug. "Join us," he said, as he released me from his embrace. He turned to Eli and shook his hand. "We can finally have that double date we talked about."

I looked up at Eli, and he shrugged and smiled, so we sat down.

"We were just about to order some food," Garrett said. Then, he seemed to remember Bridget. He turned toward her. "Bridget, this is my friend Ella and her boyfriend Elijah." He turned toward us. "Guys, this is Bridget."

She extended her hand. "Nice to meet you."

I wanted to swat her hand away, but instead, I shook it, as did Eli. "You too," I managed to squeak out. I remembered what Eli said at the Gathering about being a physical bridge and tried to adjust my attitude. I didn't want to give him more reason to suspect I was meant to bridge with Garrett, whatever that meant. "What's your major?" I asked in an attempt to be friendly.

"Oh, I haven't decided yet," she responded.

I darted my eyes at Garrett, thinking he'd started dating a freshman who may be underage.

He laughed at me. "She started as a liberal arts major a few years ago, but decided she wanted something more specific. She just hasn't figured out what yet," he explained.

Bridget smiled at him and leaned in for a kiss.

I averted my eyes.

"What about you guys?" she asked us.

"Oh, I graduated several years ago," Eli responded, as though he was an old man.

"Eli is an environmental lawyer, and I'm majoring in biology," I provided.

Finally, the waitress came and took our orders. When she dropped off the beers a few minutes later, I lifted mine for cheers with Garrett out of habit. We clinked the necks together and both took a long drink. We chatted during our meal, mostly about classes and professors. Garrett took the opportunity to give me a hard time about Brandon.

"Oh, I took one of his classes a few semesters ago," Bridget noted. "He's probably the most eligible professor on campus." She laughed, and I laughed with her.

Eli's ears perked up. "Wait, isn't this the professor that kissed you? You didn't mention he was good looking," he frowned.

I cupped his face in my palm. "Don't you worry. He doesn't hold a candle to you."

Garrett took a large drink of his beer and signaled the waitress for another. Bridget excused herself to go outside for a smoke, and I was surprised Garrett didn't join her.

"I'm trying to quit," he explained.

The three of us sat in awkward silence until Eli's phone rang. He looked at who was calling, then looked at me. "I have to take this." His eyes darted between me and Garret, worry creasing his brow. Then, he turned to Garrett and said, "Keep an eye on her while I'm gone, will you?" He left the table before Garrett could answer.

I watched him until he passed through the door into the night air.

"You okay?" Garrett asked.

I turned my attention back to him. "Of course I'm okay. Why do you ask?"

"You seem distracted. And not just by Elijah," he said.

I had forgotten how intuitive he could be. "There's just a lot going on right now," I said, as I glanced back at the door.

"You love him, don't you?" Garrett asked.

When I looked back at him to answer, I saw some of the light had left his eyes. They looked a bit clouded. I shivered despite the warm atmosphere of the bar. "Yes. Very much so," I answered.

Garrett sat up straighter. "Well, I'm happy for you," he smiled. He sounded like he meant it, but he also sounded a bit disappointed.

Bridget came back to the table, smelling of cigarettes and perfume, then our food came just as Eli got back to the table, worry on his face.

"What's wrong?" I asked.

"Our case was moved to another judge. I need to go into work and rework our arguments," he explained.

"Oh."

"Yeah." Eli looked lost. He didn't know what to do. He was torn between keeping me safe and fulfilling his

Nymph duties by doing everything he could to ensure he would win his case.

"It's fine. I'll be okay for a few hours."

He didn't share my sentiment, looking at Garrett somewhat expectantly. It took Garrett a minute to catch on.

"Oh, yeah, sure," he said. "I'll get her home."

"Thanks Garrett. I really owe you one," Eli said.

Garrett looked a little perplexed. I was sure he thought Eli was being overbearing by not letting me be out on my own, but it didn't look like he was going to say anything about it. Eli leaned down and gave me a long kiss before making a quick exit. After he left, we ate mostly in silence.

As it became darker outside and the crowd in the bar thickened, the sound system was turned up, and a song came on that excited Bridget.

"Oh, I love this song! Can we dance?" she asked Garrett.

"Sure," Garrett told her.

They headed to the dance floor, hand in hand. As I watched them dance, I could tell Garrett wasn't as carefree as he usually was when he danced. He kept glancing back at me, likely sensing that I was upset, and not paying very much attention to Bridget. She wasn't very happy about that. At one point, she grabbed his face and turned it toward her so that she could plant a rather sloppy kiss on him, as though she were staking her territory. He tried to pay better attention to her after that, and they stayed on the dance floor for a few more songs before I saw Garrett lean into Bridget and whisper something in her ear. She glared over at me, and I could see her mouth the word 'fine' before Garrett started walking away from her and toward me.

"You ready to get out of here?" he asked.

"Sure. What about Bridget?"

"I told her I was going to take you home and that I'd see her tomorrow. I didn't think you were feeling too good."

He was right. I wasn't feeling very well. Being under constant surveillance was taking a toll. I needed time to just *be*. I was grateful Eli left me in Garrett's hands rather than sending another Nymph to keep an eye on me. To spend time with someone who wasn't anticipating an attack at any given moment would be a welcome relief.

As Garrett escorted me out the door, Austin and Emma were coming in. When I started to say hi, Emma hooked her arm into Austin's and hurried away from me. I sighed. Seemed she didn't want to be near me in case it would put her in harm's way.

"That was weird," Garrett commented when we stepped outside into the crisp evening air.

"I guess she's just too wrapped up in Austin to bother with pleasantries," I reasoned.

We walked the rest of the way in silence. Garrett kept looking at me as though he wanted to say something but never did. I did my best to enjoy the breeze on my face and take in the smell of the decaying leaves scattered across the lawns of campus. When we reached my floor and Garrett was opening the stairwell door for me, I didn't feel like going home. I realized my issue hadn't been that I wanted some alone time, but rather, I wanted some carefree time. Time to relax and be myself and have fun.

"Actually, could we maybe go to your place? Beers and a movie?"

"You sure Eli wouldn't mind?" he asked.

I rolled my eyes and started up the stairs to his floor. When he opened the door to his apartment, I was hit with a blast of wintery air. "Is your heater broken?"

Garrett walked over to his thermostat and started adjusting it. "Just wasn't expecting company is all."

"You mean, you keep it this cold on purpose?"

"You know I don't get cold easily. Plus, you know, cost savings." He went into his bedroom and came out with a thick linen blanket, which he threw at me.

I settled myself into his couch and turned on his TV, searching for a movie to watch while he grabbed a couple beers from the fridge before joining me. He stole the remote from me when he sat down and put on a comedy.

"I think you could use a laugh," he noted.

We watched the first few minutes of the movie, but I was having a hard time shutting my brain off. "Do you have any pot?"

He was taken completely off guard. "You smoke?!"

"Just pot. And only occasionally."

"How do I not know this about you? Jesus, Ella." He got up and went into the kitchen. I was trying not to laugh at his reaction. He returned a few minutes later with a couple joints, an ashtray, a lighter, and an assortment of snacks.

"I can always count on you," I told him. He smiled and handed me a joint, and I leaned toward him as he lit it for me.

"Have I seen you high before?" he wondered.

I started nodding as I held the smoke in. I let it swirl through my lungs, and just when I thought they might collapse, I exhaled. "Yes, a few times," I told him. "I think you always assumed I was drunk."

I could feel the tightness in my chest that I hadn't realized was there start to loosen. I took another large hit and passed it to Garrett. Our hands touched as he took it from me, and I felt electrified. The surge started in my fingertips and shot all the way to my toes. Garrett gave me a long look before putting the joint to his mouth. "This is nuts," he said.

I leaned my head on his shoulder. He smelled woodsy with a hint of something sweet. "For the record, I didn't know for sure that you smoked, either."

It wasn't long before the body buzz hit me, and I realized Garrett had some pretty strong stuff. Much stronger than what Owen ever had.

"You should hook Owen up with your supplier. Yours is way better than his."

"Owen smokes too? My life is a lie!" he exclaimed.

I tilted my head up at him, and he was looking down at me with a half smirk, indicating he was purposefully being overdramatic. Sitting there, up against him, it felt right. It was familiar and safe. For the first time in a while—outside of when I was with Eli—I felt content.

"Any other secrets about your life you want to share while we're at it?" he asked, sounding hopeful.

I considered for a moment. "There are plenty of secrets I'd like to share, but I'm not going to."

"Oh, yeah. Same," he said while nodding.

I laughed and smacked him in the stomach. It felt like my arm was moving twice as fast as usual. My entire body felt like it was hovering. I looked around the room and noticed the blues of the wall looked bluer. It made me think about Garrett's eyes.

I got up and turned the TV off, which he protested, then turned on the stereo and cranked it up. I came back to the couch, stood over him, and searched his eyes. I noticed how incredibly clear blue they were. More so than normal.

I pulled the joint from his mouth, took another hit, then set it in the ashtray.

"Let's dance," I said. I grabbed his hands and pulled him up and over near the stereo. At first, he just stood and watched me. I was sure I looked like a fool, but I felt the beat of the music and danced with it anyway. Eventually, he joined me, and we danced for what felt like hours with occasional trips back to the coffee table for another hit.

At one point, my hand accidentally brushed against the only plant he had in the room, and it grew a little and started to bud. I was pretty sure he wouldn't notice. After a while, we settled back on the couch.

We stayed up for several hours talking about nothing and eating the snacks he had brought out. We started throwing pretzel nuggets at each other to see who could catch one in their mouth. I did not do so well at that.

When I woke up the next morning, I was surprised to find myself still on Garrett's couch. I was snuggled into his shoulder, and his head was resting on top of mine. His arm was around me, holding me in place.

"What time is it?" he asked when I started to get up, his voice gravelly from having just woken.

"I have no idea," I admitted.

He finally opened his eyes and quickly pulled his arm out from behind me.

I stood and stretched. "I should get going," I told him. "Thanks for last night. I needed that."

He walked me to the door. "We should do it again soon," he said.

I started down the hallway.

"Hey, Ella?"

I turned back toward him.

"I'm not sure what's going on with you, but you know you can come here anytime you need to get away, right?"

I smiled and said thanks, then headed to my apartment. Owen was pacing the floor when I came in.

"Emma came looking for you last night. She said she saw you leave the bar with Garrett?"

"Yeah, Eli had a work emergency, so he left me in Garrett's care," I explained.

"And you're just now getting home?"

"It was late, and I was tired. We fell asleep. And I needed a break from the constant surveillance anyway."

"Elijah texted me last night and said he was going to sleep at the office and asked if I could come over and stay with you for the night. Imagine my surprise when I got here, and you weren't home."

"I'm sorry if I made you worry." I didn't know what else to say.

"Worry? I was downright panicked! I almost called Aaron and Armeta a million times last night. You could have at least texted!"

"Look, Owen, I didn't intend on falling asleep there, and I came home as soon as I woke up. Now, if you'll excuse me, I need a shower." I didn't mean to be short with him, but he was getting on my nerves.

When I emerged from the bathroom a short time later, Owen had made breakfast and handed me a coffee. "Peace offering?" he said.

"I'm not the one that was angry," I told him.

Owen shrugged, and we sat down to eat. While I was shoveling eggs into my mouth, he asked about Halloween. "Are we going to the costume party at the bar?"

"I hadn't given it much thought."

"Sounds like you could use a social event."

"I mean, it could be fun," I considered.

"Then, let's do it."

***

In the days leading up to Halloween, life went on as usual. Eli won his big case, and after he came home from celebrating with his firm, we had our own private celebration. The Relay for Life event came and went without incident. We collected enough supplies for the women's shelter to hold them over until the end of the year. Emma stopped showing up to work at that point, so I had to deliver the supplies to the shelter on my own. It took several trips, but all of the residents were very grateful. The kids were especially excited since there were several new toys and books.

With no more large events to worry about for work, I was able to focus on schoolwork and finished my paper on Sirens for Mythology. There hadn't been any more reports of Nymphs going missing since the one we heard about the morning Garrett caught me in a towel, and we hadn't seen anyone suspicious around me, so the Elders called back most of the volunteer guards who had been following me everywhere, much to Aaron and Armeta's dismay.

When Halloween finally arrived, I was excited to have some fun after such a stressful month. Eli and I arrived at the bar just as the sun was setting. The place was packed already. We went inside and found our way to Owen and Garrett, pushing past plenty of zombies, vampires, and nurses.

Owen was dressed as a woodland elf, complete with a long-haired wig, fake pointy ears, and green tights.

"Really? An elf?" I teased him.

"I needed a reason to wear tights!" he joked, already a little drunk by the sound of it.

"That's just offensive," Garrett commented.

"Yeah? And what are you supposed to be?" Owen asked him.

Garrett held his arms out wide as if he were gesturing to the obvious. "I'm a werewolf. See the fangs?" he said, baring his teeth. "I come by the hair naturally," he quipped, stroking his short beard before turning his attention to me. "What the hell are you, Ella? Sexy Tinkerbell?"

"Tinkerbell?" I questioned while looking down at my costume. I could see why he would have thought that. The mini-skirt I was wearing was made to look like leaves with a choppy hem. The top was a dark green Victorian mid-bust corset, and I had constructed myself a crown made of twigs and ribbons.

"I'm a Nymph, Garrett," I proclaimed. "Isn't it obvious?"

Eli chuckled, and Owen burst out laughing causing the beer that he was about to swallow to spew out into the crowd. Several people turned to give him a dirty look.

Garrett looked over my costume once more. His eyes lingered a little too long, admiring how much lift it provided my breasts. He tore his eyes away and addressed Eli, "I guess that makes you her Satyr?" he asked, pointing toward the horns on his head.

"I told you people would jump to that conclusion," Eli told me. "I'm supposed to be a devil."

"Where's Bridget?" I asked.

"She had to work," Garrett shrugged.

"Has anyone seen Emma?" I asked, looking around at the crowd.

Owen frowned. "She isn't coming. She said she had better plans with Austin."

"Who needs her!" Garrett said.

Eli clapped his hand on Owen's shoulder in a show of support, then went to get us drinks from the bar. We stayed for a few hours, talking, drinking, and dancing. I almost forgot about the unknown monster out there searching for me. Almost.

When we decided to call it a night, Owen went to find Garrett, who had wandered off a bit ago. Eli and I headed outside to wait for them, but right outside the doors was crowded with smokers, so I headed across the street to wait.

That decision changed my life.

Eli was standing halfway out the door still, trying to see if Owen and Garrett were on their way yet.

A car turned the corner toward me when my foot left the curb. I didn't notice it start to speed up.

There was a small ruckus in the smoker crowd that caused Eli to turn his head back to me. "Ella!" he yelled.

I heard the anguish in his voice and quickly turned to him. He left the doorway and had just gotten to the curb.

That was when I noticed the car.

The smoker crowd started screaming.

I braced for impact. Before I knew it, I was shoved out of the way, landing hard on the pavement. I watched in horror as the car struck Eli, and he flew several feet through the air. The car squealed around the next corner and out of sight. I scrambled to my feet and ran to Eli.

The crowd of smokers were screaming for help. A few had their phones out, and I hoped they were calling 911. I kneeled down beside Eli, ignoring the screaming pain in my knee. He was moaning and bleeding from a large wound on his head.

"Eli! Eli, can you hear me?"

His response was barely a whisper. "Ella."

"Eli," I choked. "It's going to be okay. Help is on the way." Tears were streaming down my face.

He winced. "They're not going to make it in time," he insisted.

"No, no, no," I said between sobs. "This isn't happening. This can't be happening."

"Ella. Listen to me."

I moved so that his head was resting in my lap, trying to make him as comfortable as possible.

"It's important. Listen."

I wiped my eyes and focused on his.

"Ella. I love you. I understand now."

"I love you too," I told him, trying to give him a smile.

"I understand my purpose. I was meant to love you. To protect you." He winced again and struggled for another breath. "This is where my life is meant to end."

"Eli, no. Don't, please," I said, my voice cracking.

"You have to stay strong. You have to move on. You are meant to be the bridge. You have to find him and know him and love him. It's vital. I just know it is. It's a force of nature. Even if I survived, we wouldn't have lasted. We would have grown apart to make room for him." He struggled to raise his hand up to my face.

I reached out and helped him the rest of the way, holding my hand over his, keeping his fingertips pressed against my cheek.

"Here," he said. "Take what's left and know that I'll be with you always."

I felt the oddest sensation then. It was almost electric, like when I rubbed the earth on my arms during the opening blessing, but much more potent.

All of a sudden, I could feel Eli's aura swimming inside me. I could feel his pain and his sorrow, but also his love and his hope. My aching knee started to feel better as I realized what was happening.

He was channeling his energy to me. The last of his life force.

Owen dropped down beside me just as Eli took his last breath, Garrett on his heels. I heard an earth-shattering scream far in the distance.

When I ran out of breath, I realized it was me

COMING SOON

Chronicles of The Foretold
BOOK 2

Awakening:

The Restoration

Follow Nikki Thornton on Social Media

Facebook

Instagram

NIKKI.THORNTON.AUTHOR

Goodreads

Amazon Author Page

Made in the USA
Columbia, SC
13 October 2023

24444281R00157